Rock, Paper, Scissors

Scissors

Tamela Miles

ISBN-10: 0692557393
ISBN-13: 978-0692557396

Written by Tamela Miles
Tamela Miles Books on Facebook
https://www.facebook.com/Tamela-Miles-Books-350618404965591/timeline/?ref=aymt_homepage_panel

Published by Broken Publications
www.BrokenPublications.com

Author photo credit:
Nichanh Nicole Photography, Torrance CA

A
Pacific Northwest
Publisher

www.BrokenPublications.com

"This is a compilation of previously written stories and some new ones. Although I had read many of the stories in this book, I enjoyed them all over again. These are stories about ghosts, witches, demons, and things that go bump in the night."

Reviewed by: Linda Tonis

Member of the Paranormal Romance Review Team

http://www.paranormalromanceguild.com/reviewstamelamiles.htm

Dedication

For Mom and Dad, who pushed me to achieve far greater than just average and are my greatest supporters... and for all that they have done, too.

For my sisters and brothers, who keep life interesting and remind me that I am never alone and we are all on the same journey.

For my besties and other friends: thank you for your friendship.

For actor Zach Galligan, for his inspiration and being a good sport.

Table of Contents

Breathe

"What the hell is this?" Tierney asked her husband, frowning at the small book she'd recovered from beneath the cushions of the brown sofa in the middle of the living room. *"Demons, Great and Small,"* she read aloud. "Rob, what is this unholy crap you were evidently hiding from me?"

Rob sighed loudly and snatched the book from his wife's hands. His blue eyes met hers and he attempted to smile but failed miserably. *Oh, God,* he thought, *not another angry tirade from her.*

His gaze traveled to the top of her long brown hair and remained there.

"It's just… a book," he trailed off lamely.

Tierney felt her temper soar to greater heights. *Please, not this demonic crap in our home again.* They were both Baptists but hadn't been to church together in years. *It's not that I lost my faith,* she justified defensively. They were both so busy these days. Tierney was a kindergarten teacher at a local elementary school and Rob slaved as a graphic designer for The Man at an office building in Downtown Los Angeles. He was also the lead guitarist for his band. Rob was, had always been, and probably would always be a rocker, in beliefs, manner, and dress. He had long black hair and wore jeans and t-shirts most of the time. She stepped closer to him, trying to meet his eyes with her worried dark brown ones.

"Throw that damn book in the garbage, Rob!" Tierney demanded angrily.

"Not a chance," Rob said fiercely, standing his ground. "It's a loaner from a friend." He tossed the book on one of the end tables next to the sofa.

Before the argument could escalate, Tierney clutched her throat, feeling another asthma attack coming on. Rob grabbed her arm in concern and reached into her jeans pocket for her inhaler. He put it to her lips and watched her struggle to breathe. After a few long moments, she was filling her lungs with air as well as she could.

"You ok?" Rob asked, stroking her hair. She nodded.

"It's not as if my soul is in danger by having this book in our house, Tierney," he said softly.

"You know, right about now I'd sell my soul to be able to breathe properly," Tierney said flippantly, smiling at her husband, anger forgotten after their bonding moment.

Rob kissed his wife's forehead gently and they stayed in a tight embrace for a few moments.

∞

Childish giggling woke Tierney almost instantly. She turned over quickly, her legs tangling with Rob's as he slept. It was well after midnight and they had been in bed for nearly an hour. She was a light sleeper and the slightest noise usually woke her up.

"Rob?" she said into the darkness. "Are you laughing?"

He grunted, untangled his legs from hers, and slept on.

The childish laughter came again from the dark and Tierney sat up in bed. Hesitant to turn on the lamp by the bed for fear of waking up Rob, she strained to see. The laughter started again, this time closer to her side of the bed and she shivered in fear. *Maybe it's coming from next door,* she told herself. Suddenly, the giggling was right next to her ear.

"Breathe," a child's voice commanded.

Tierney felt her heart plummet to her to her stomach but took a deep breath. God, she could breathe much easier. She waited for her airway to constrict for a few long, tense moments, but nothing happened. She took another breath and marveled at the sudden ease of her breathing.

Suddenly, Rob turned over onto his back, shuddering and gasping for air. He clutched his throat. Tierney switched on the lamp quickly.

"Rob?!" she yelled, trying to wrestle his hands from his throat. She leaned over him. His eyes were open and tearing up. She was up and running for the phone in an instant and dialed

911. After giving emergency services her address and explaining the situation, she dashed back to the bed.

"Can't breathe," Rob managed to say between gasps.

Tierney had never felt so helpless in her entire life. She watched as her husband of five years fought for air and tears rolled down her face. Seemingly from nowhere, a dark suspicion crossed her mind as she remembered the childish voice whispering in her ear. Now Rob – who had never had trouble breathing – was dying, and she was breathing just fine for the first time in her life. She shivered in terror. She cradled Rob in her arms, telling him that help was on the way and to hold on for her, for them.

"Love you always," Rob said softly, panting. His eyes met hers and he stared at her intently before closing them and going limp in her arms. She heard the ambulance siren in their driveway and rushed from the bedroom to open the front door.

Demons are never far from us, so be careful what you say, she thought darkly. Sometimes, they lie in wait for humankind to deliver gifts that cost much more than we are willing to pay. Sometimes, the cost is a soul.

One

"It's all in the telling," Ethan said softly, positioning the phone between his chin and shoulder. He smiled to himself, imagining his best friend, Anya, seated at the black desk in her bedroom, idly chewing a pen cap to death.

"Are you chewing a pen?" Ethan asked suddenly.

Anya paused, startled by his accuracy. She laughed into the phone before answering.

"Yes. How did you know? Do you have hidden cameras in my bedroom? Perv."

"No," Ethan answered, amused. "Nothing like that." He pictured her long dark hair spilling across her shoulders and her brown eyes filled with laughter and some deep sadness that was a breathing, vital part of her.

Anya James had been a substantial part of his life since high school. She was the only girl who had ever dared to strike up a conversation with him, a socially challenged misfit who wasn't particularly smart or handsome. Stories had drawn them together and they had remained that way for many years.

Anya interrupted his train of thought.

"You're right, Ethan. It's all about how you craft the story. We need to revisit character development. I don't think that the opening scene is going to work as well as we had hoped. I'll work on it tonight and call you tomorrow after class."

"Cool," Ethan said. "Talk to you tomorrow."

Ethan Fallows hung up and rolled over onto his back on his narrow futon. He was tall and lanky and his feet dangled over the edge. He didn't really mind it because he was comfortable. He wasn't comfortable with his friendship with Anya, however. He felt tortured every time they spoke on the phone or hung out because he was desperately in love with her. He faked a smile whenever she brought up one of her many boyfriends and swallowed the lump in his throat, listening intently to her joys and sorrows.

Ethan swept his long, dark hair away from his face and crossed his arms on his chest. *There's a way to tip the scales in my favor,* he reminded himself. *Just do it a few more times and let's see what happens,* he thought. Suddenly, he sat and pushed himself up from the futon. He moved over to his old wooden desk and opened the bottom drawer. His heart began to beat a little faster as he picked up a small black box.

∞

Anya rolled over in her big bed, her thoughts keeping her awake. She was unsettled and couldn't stop this feeling of impending trouble. She hadn't been sleeping well for the last few nights and that only seemed to make the feeling more intense. *Hell is full of insomniacs,* she thought wryly, putting a pillow over her head to block out the moonlight.

Her thoughts turned to her pillar of strength, Ethan. They had been best friends for five years this Christmas and if this was to be their last holiday season as friends for whatever reason, she would still be grateful for all the good he had brought to her life. He was one of the good guys. She was glad that the whole sex thing was behind them now, of course. They had slept together one time during their junior year in high school and both had agreed that some things were better left to the imagination. It hadn't been a horrible experience and Ethan had been an inventive lover.... What he lacked in sexual experience he made up for in passion, but Anya loved him and cherished his friendship too much to use him. With all that long, black hair and pale skin, he would make some girl really happy one day.

Anya lived in Caddo, a little town in Northern California, and had been there from the time she was a toddler. Her family had moved from Pasadena when her mom, Stephanie, was pregnant with her younger brother, Chris. She couldn't imagine living anywhere else because her parents had created the perfect life in this small town. Her house was beautiful and her parents' high school graduation gift had been the Honda parked in the driveway. She and Ethan were second year college students at the local community college, both English majors. They had been writing stories as a hobby since the beginning of their friendship and creating together had only cemented their bond.

Anya moved into a more comfortable position, her mind finally at peace. She smiled, feeling herself beginning to drift off. She had nothing to complain about.

∞

It began as a buzzing in her mind. Static was the only way that Anya could describe the noise going on inside of her head when she was seated at the kitchen table across from her younger brother, Chris. She had just taken a bite of toast and, suddenly, that weird buzzing started. Ignoring it seemed to be her only option.

"What was the slut with a thousand sex partners doing at home last night?" Chris asked snidely. A red cap covered his dark, messy hair and his jeans hung loosely from his frame.

"Doing college level homework. Not that you'll ever see the inside of a college classroom after you graduate, Chris," Anya replied smartly. "*If* you graduate."

"Shut up, prostitute," Chris fired back angrily. He stood up abruptly to take his plate to the sink and tripped over his own foot. Anya snickered.

"Dumbass," she said breezily, watching his final glare as he grabbed his backpack and left the kitchen, presumably on his way to drink beer with his loser friends on one of the back roads in Caddo instead of going to school.

"You shouldn't let him talk to you like that, Anya. Your brother has a problem with respect."

Anya whipped around in her chair, expecting to see her dad standing in the doorway. There was no one there. "Dad?" she called out. No one answered. She shrugged it off after a moment, rinsing her plate in the sink. A memory from last night's dream that she had struggled to recover this morning in bed flashed into her mind. In the dream, she had been stretched out on her bed with Ethan on top of her. His long hair hung loose around his face and he was kissing her.

"Weird," Anya said to herself. Sex dreams about Ethan could never be a good thing, she decided, laughing the whole thing away. Still, the buzzing in her mind continued.

∞

Anya and Ethan were seated across from each other in the cafeteria, their plastic plates and soda cans pushed to the side of the table. The place was humming with activity as students exchanged hurried goodbyes on their way to their next classes.

"Sleeping better these days?" Ethan inquired, laying one long leg on the empty chair.

Anya smiled tiredly.

"Sadly, no. I used to be dead to the world as soon as my head hit the pillow, but now…" she trailed off. She rested her chin in her hand, shaking her head. "And my love life sucks right now, as my little brother pointed out this morning."

Ethan grinned. "Ah, yes. More tidbits of wisdom from the idiot, Chris." His gaze moved away from hers to just above her head and he licked his lips. He appeared to be in deep thought. "Chris has a real respect problem," he said softly.

Anya blinked in astonishment, leaning forward on the table. "My dad said the same thing this morning. Chris and I have always been at war." She rolled her eyes.

Ethan rubbed his stubbled chin and gave her a warm smile. "You need to craft your life just like we craft our stories, Anya. Your life is like a story, slowly unfolding from one day to the next, but you maintain control over the main character. You need to shape things to be the way that you want them, not wait around on some mythical predetermined course of events to make your decisions for you. Fate is what you make it."

Anya nodded. "Yes, I agree. I have sort of taken my hands off the wheel when it comes to my life. I'm guilty of drifting. Ever since I broke things off with my last boyfriend, I've just been drifting from one day to the next, I guess." She shrugged. "I suppose I really was in love."

She stood up, grabbing the handle of her rolling bag. "Gotta run, Ethan. I'll be late for class. Call me tonight?"

Ethan nodded, rising to his feet. He caught Anya in his arms, hugging her fiercely. He kissed the top of her head. "Things will get better. You'll see, everything will be as it should be again soon," he whispered. She kissed his cheek and headed out of the cafeteria with a wave.

As Anya walked, the buzzing returned, louder and more insistent. She paused and rubbed her forehead. "It's all in the telling," a voice said in her mind, chuckling. She turned around quickly, expecting to see Ethan directly behind her. He wasn't there, just as her dad hadn't been there in the kitchen earlier. *But I heard his voice so clearly,* she thought to herself, heading down one of the concrete paths to class.

∞

By 5:00 that afternoon, Anya was sure that she was losing her mind. The buzzing had turned into an incessant drone of voices that sounded like the thoughts of others intruding in her mind. Some voices, like Chris, she recognized and the others were unfamiliar. The whole situation was beyond frightening and she remained curled up in a fetal position on the middle of her bed.

She was alone in the house as the tears fell down her face and she shivered, afraid of what would come next. Chris could be anywhere in Caddo and her parents were both still at work. She considered calling Ethan, but what could she say besides she was losing her mind? *I'm really sick,* she thought, panicking.

"You could pick up the phone and call but that's really unnecessary, Anya," Ethan's voice said clearly in her head, set apart from the drone of other voices. "I'm right here. Talk to me."

Anya jerked into a sitting position. "Ethan's voice in my head?" she whispered aloud to herself. "That's it. I'm definitely going crazy." She pushed her hair out of her face and wiped her damp cheeks with her hands.

17

Ethan's voice came again. "No, you're not. Technically, the bonding does create some weird side effects that could be seen by some as schizophrenia, but you're quite sane. I established this mind bond between us so you would never be alone."

Without thinking, she answered him. "You're not real. None of this is real except the schizophrenic part. I have lost my mind and probably need to be on meds, which scares me. My head is making up Ethan so I feel safe. Please stop talking." She drew her knees up and rested her forehead on them, rocking back and forth on the bed.

"Oh, the bond is quite real," Ethan responded calmly. "I've been working on it for days and, except for the other voices in your mind, it's perfect. And permanent." He sounded cheerful. "You need me, Anya, and now you'll never be without me." He paused and she heard a deep sigh. "Can you imagine what life would have been like in high school if we were bonded then?"

"A living hell," Anya snapped angrily. She knew there was no point in getting angry and frustrated with her own brain, but it felt good to yell at imaginary Ethan. She knew she needed help but was afraid to drive herself to the hospital and decided to wait for her parents to get home. Another thought came to her. What if this *was* real? What if Ethan really had done this to her? She believed in demons and dark forces. She believed they could wreak havoc with your life if you let them in.

"You'll get used to the other voices in time. Trust me, Anya."

"Ethan, is this bonding a spell of some kind?" she said abruptly. "Demon worship, maybe?"

"The dark serves my purpose sometimes," Ethan replied nonchalantly. "Sleep, Anya. Close your eyes and rest."

The multitude of other voices became loud in her head again and she pounded her forehead with both hands in a futile attempt to make them stop. She rested on her bed in the dark, but Ethan didn't come back.

∞

Anya remembered the look of horrified fear on her mother's face as she told her about the voices in her head later that evening. She'd come into the kitchen and found her daughter on the kitchen floor sobbing while holding a large knife. The voices had only become more clamorous in the few hours since she'd last heard Ethan's voice. Half of her needed someone to blame, so she clung to the belief that this mind bond was some sort of spell that could be broken. Maybe if Ethan died....

"I have to call Hud," Stephanie said, holding onto Anya's hand with one of her own and reaching in her coat pocket for her cell phone with the other.

"No! Don't tell Dad. Just get me to the psych ward, Mama. Please."

Now, Anya rested in a bed in the psychiatric ward of the hospital, full of psychotropic drugs. She was floating and the voices in her mind were a slight murmur. She saw her mother's face appear in the small window of the door to her room and gave her a weary smile. Stephanie smiled back with watery eyes and disappeared again.

Anya looked down at the hospital gown, fighting back tears of her own. She felt calm, even rational. There was no formal diagnosis yet, but she had heard her doctor discussing the likely probability of schizophrenia with her mother in the hallway outside of her room. It made so much more sense than that mind bond imaginary Ethan had been talking about.

"I'll take my meds every day and everything will be just the way it was," Anya told herself quietly. She even mustered another smile. "You're gonna be okay."

"What in the hell have you done?" Ethan's voice thundered in her mind.

Anya was immediately terrified. She rubbed her temples, her lips parting in a silent scream. *Oh, God, he's here again!* She honestly thought that she had heard the last from imaginary Ethan. "What... what do you mean?"

"I can't hear your thoughts clearly anymore. Where are you?" His voice sounded suspicious.

"I'm sick, Ethan. I know I shouldn't hear your imaginary voice or anyone else's in my mind. I'm in the psych ward, completely drugged up. Please shut up now."

"Damn it!" he shouted. There was a note of desperation in his voice beneath the anger. "Anya, don't take the pills. Those kinds of pills weaken the bond and make it difficult for me to find you in my head."

"Screw you," Anya retorted. "I'm taking these pills as long as I have to because I hate the sound of your voice. You're not even real and I hate you."

"Anya, I love you. I have always loved you," Ethan said softly, coldly. "The bonding can make you very happy or bring the worst kind of hell. If you keep taking those pills, I'll find a way to make it worse, I promise you that. I'll do anything to keep you. You decide."

"To hell with you," Anya yelled.

"Okay, I see. You need persuading. I can get rid of your parents and I know where to find your brother, too. Oh, I can kill them all, no problem," he threatened in a teasing voice.

"Get out of my head!" Anya shouted, pounding her forehead with her hand.

"I'll leave you alone to make up your mind," Ethan said.

A nurse came into Anya's room a moment later, holding a small cup of pills. She rubbed her back, trying to calm her down. The nurse poured her a cup of water and handed her the small paper cup of pills. Anya put them all into her mouth and swallowed the water in one gulp. When the nurse left, she stealthily spit them into her open hand and put them under her pillow.

Anya was torn between firm belief in diseases of the mind and diseases of the soul. If she was soul sick and Ethan was to blame, she couldn't risk her family's lives. If Ethan could pull this off, what the hell else could he do? Better not to take the chance. She vowed that if he had made some dark deal with demons in exchange for this power, he would pay. Curse his filthy, black heart, he would pay for this.

"Who's my little girl?" Ethan whispered in her mind, intruding on her thoughts.

"I am. I love you, Ethan," Anya whispered back woodenly.

∞

Ethan placed the black wooden box on his desk and lifted the top. He pulled out strands of Anya's hair, one of her earrings she'd thought she lost, and a small picture of the two of them taken last Christmas. He caressed her face in the picture, remembering that Christmas and all of the ones before. He put the picture down with the other things in the chalk circle he'd made on his hardwood floor.

He lit the candles on his desk and bowed his head, closing his eyes. "Spirits, work thy will. I submit to your will and I ask humbly that you renew the bond between me and Anya James. Until death, we are one."

Ethan picked up a small pocket knife and slashed the palm of his hand, allowing his blood to drip into the chalk circle. All of the windows in his room were closed, but a sharp wind blew the candles out. He smiled in the darkness.

∞

"Jarrod, are you going to help me or not?" Anya asked, exasperation in her voice. She was on the phone with a friend that she had dated back in high school, and the conversation had suddenly become circular. She was asking for help and he wanted to know why.

"Why do you need a Wiccan's help?"

Anya sighed impatiently. There was no way that she was telling him that the voices in her head quite possibly were the result of meticulous spell casting by an even older friend. *Ethan Fallows, damn you,* she cursed inwardly. "I told you, I need as much information about witchcraft as possible for this story I'm working on with Ethan."

That seemed to allay Jarrod's suspicions and he went on to give her the name of a practicing Wiccan who also read tarot cards in the Caddo area. Her name was Catarina and she had a small Wiccan shop in the Crossroads Mall. Anya remembered seeing the shop, called Aware, in passing many times, but she had never stopped in. She was not one for tarot readings and all that creepy stuff. She smiled grimly to herself, hanging up the phone. What could possibly be creepier than the trouble she was in now?

Anya hadn't seen Ethan since she was released from the psych ward a month before. Imaginary Ethan, however, spoke in her mind almost every day. No amount of medication that she had been given upon her release could make him or the din of voices in her mind go away completely. There was always a buzz, a murmuring of different voices.

It was good to be home and out of sweat pants. She had worn comfortable, shabby clothes in the hospital and she felt like shouting with joy as she looked down at the blue jeans and tight beige sweater she wore today. She decided that she was perfectly dressed for lunch with Ethan and meeting up with Jarrod later on, after she ran to the mall, of course. Meeting with Catarina was her top priority right now. If there was a way to stop Ethan, if he was doing this, she wanted in.

∞

"Did you take your pills last night before bed?" Anya's mother, Stephanie, asked as she eyed her daughter with obvious concern. Anya was an almost perfect copy of Stephanie, a feisty middle-aged brunette.

Anya huffed. "Yes, Mom, I take my pills every day. Really, I'm much better now. The voices are pretty much gone now. Me being sick, it was like… a trivial sneeze." She kissed her mother's cheek impulsively after the lie left her lips. After all that had happened, Anya found that she had a greater appreciation for her family. Even Chris, her dunce of a brother.

"I'm having lunch with Ethan and going to the movies with Jarrod. Bye, Mom."

Anya headed out the door and into the day's cold air. Caddo wasn't far enough north for snowfall, but the rain during the winter was more than an occasional thunder storm. Luckily, it wasn't a rainy day, and as she walked to her sporty Honda in the driveway, she enjoyed the afternoon sun on her skin.

∞

The short drive from Anya's house to the Crossroads Mall was uneventful. She had expected to hear imaginary Ethan in her head, shouting a warning to keep her situation secret, but that didn't happen. She parked her car in the large lot and walked through the mall to the Wiccan shop, Aware. She prayed the whole way that Catarina was as good as Jarrod had said. Jarrod was definitely more than a little fascinated with all things occult.

"Hi. Welcome to Aware." A young woman with strikingly black hair and a happy smile greeted Anya as she walked into the store.

"Hi. Are you Catarina?"

Catarina nodded and extended a hand. Anya shook it, grateful that she may not be alone in this anymore. "Someone put a spell on me and I want the bastard to pay," she blurted out.

The young witch frowned. "Are you seeing things you shouldn't be seeing?"

"Hearing them," Anya said quickly. "Voices in my head all day long. He talks to me in my head, too."

"Let's go to the back and see what I can do for you," Catarina said decisively, pulling the main gate to the store down and locking it. "I'll need a personal item from you."

∞

Catarina turned the small diamond earring over in her hands. "He's strong," she noted. "What he has set up around you is in no way a good thing."

They sat at a table in the small back room, scented candles providing dim light and a pleasant smell. Jars filled with various powders crowded the top shelves and tons of books took up room on the lower shelves.

"There's at least one demon doing his bidding, and as long as he keeps sacrificing something... well, they'll continue to torment you with this mental bond. Was he a lover?"

"Ethan was a friend. We only slept together once, years ago. I didn't know he would go to this extreme to try to get me back in bed." Anya looked up nervously. "Can you help? Can you break the bond?"

"It won't be an easy undertaking, but I think I can do it," Catarina said, laying the earring down and taking Anya's hands in both of hers. "You should know that if I free you, the demons will torment Ethan instead, possibly until he dies."

Anya imagined Ethan's head filled with voices, the simplest task almost impossible for him to do. She thought of her own situation and how little he seemed to care about her welfare as long as she was his possession. She was tired of telling him how much she loved him and the mind bond he had created.

"Let's do this," she said firmly.

If she was wrong and she really was schizophrenic, nothing would happen to Ethan.

∞

They were standing in the center of a chalk circle on the floor, surrounding by many glowing candles. Catarina chanted musically, sprinkling some mysterious moss green powder in Anya's long dark hair.

"Bind Ethan Fallows from doing harm. Bind the power of one," Catarina said, then went back to chanting.

Anya's stomach fluttered nervously and she closed her eyes, anticipating some change in the murmuring in her mind. When it finally came, she felt a release from the band of pressure that had been surrounding her head for weeks. The whispers stopped and there was blessed silence in her head.

"I'm free! Thank God, I'm finally free," she said softly in wonder.

Catarina smiled serenely and pulled Anya into a brief, tight embrace.

∞

Ethan believed he was surely in hell. A few moments ago, he'd been preparing for his lunch date with Anya when a swell of voices filled his head. He clutched his forehead in shock, willing them to go away. What had he done wrong with the magick? These voices were to subdue Anya, make her more docile and accepting. The only thing that could stop him was a spiritual counter strike from someone whose power matched his own. That must be it. The ungrateful bitch had help. He whispered a few words and the voices became a dull hum in the back of his mind.

He wondered if she had the balls to face him for lunch today after this. He would be at Baby Q's to restore order to the bond. Damn right he would be there.

∞

Anya sat at a table in the back of Baby Q's restaurant, looking forward to a meal for the first time in weeks. A rib sandwich sounded perfect and her stomach growled. She smiled to herself. Not a single voice. She wondered if her happiness was premature. Catarina had warned her that Ethan may strike again and had given her a cell phone number in case the need to see her again should arise.

Ethan entered the restaurant and looked around for a moment. Spotting Anya, he headed toward the table.

"Anya," he said evenly, his tone neutral.

Anya realized that the name of the game was cat and mouse, so she responded in kind.

"Ethan, good to see you. Thanks for joining me for lunch today." She smiled sweetly. "I've really missed you." The look on his face was priceless.

After eating, they talked for a while about her return to the local community college in the spring and new stories they had been working on while they were apart. He told her about the persistent rumors circulating in their small social circle about her illness. Anya kept the same cloying look on her face and neither confirmed nor denied.

Suddenly, he spoke clearly in her mind. "You think you can stop me, don't you? This is just a temporary setback."

Anya was dismayed but dared not show it. She answered in her mind. "How did you like those voices in your head, Ethan?"

Aloud, he said, "Are you sure you're feeling better?"

She responded aloud. "I'm great, Ethan. Really. Thanks for asking." Inside, she was panicking. She had to get the hell out of there and call Catarina. She looked at her watch. "Time flies and all that, so I have to run. We'll do this again sometime soon, Ethan." Surprised by her composure, she actually leaned down and kissed his cheek. "See ya." She headed for the entrance to Baby Q's and left without looking back. She left him with the bill.

Anya sat in her car in the restaurant parking lot and debated whether or not to call Catarina at the moment. She decided against it and made the decision to call from the safety of home. She had to get as far away from Ethan as possible.

∞

Later, around dusk, Ethan stood in the chalk circle, pocket knife in hand. Black candles were lit on his desk. He slashed the knife across the palm of his hand, letting blood drip into the circle. *So, Anya wants to play games,* he thought. She would learn a few new things about him by the time he was done.

"Renew the bond between Anya James and me," Ethan demanded. A sharp breeze kicked up and one of the candles winked out. He smiled darkly. This next series of spells would require a small animal….

∞

"This might actually work," Catarina said, tapping one of the spells in a huge, ancient book. "If we're successful, Ethan may never be free of the demons that he summoned."

Anya nodded in understanding, thinking to herself that she didn't give a rat's ass about Ethan, her best friend of many years turned captor. Ethan establishing a mind bond with her by using spells had pretty much ended their friendship permanently. At the worst, she heard a never ending stream of conversations in her head that made it almost impossible to concentrate on anything. Sometimes, he would speak in her mind. This had been going on for months and Anya had come to Catarina, the Wiccan, for help.

"However you do it is okay with me. Just please make him stop," Anya said anxiously, adjusting the strap of her denim overalls. Catarina had instructed her to wear comfy clothing because they would be working in the back room of Aware, the magick shop where Catarina worked. She wore a long black cotton dress that perfectly matched her black hair. They had spent the past two hours looking through just about every book to find a spell that would end Ethan's madness.

Catarina gestured and Anya came over to peer at the book with her. She couldn't understand everything except for a few key words that sounded ominous. "So, we're going to do another binding spell to keep him from harming me and do this other spell, as well?" Anya asked.

"Yes," she answered. "By the time we're through with Ethan, he'll be crazier than a bag of cats. Imagine your suffering, but ten times worse." She frowned. "The only thing that bothers me is that you're going to have to get close to him again. You need to make him think that you're fine now, gain his trust. Make him think that he's imagining this mind bond with you."

Anya smiled brightly, feeling the band of nervous tension around her neck ease up. She had a feeling that she knew where Catarina was going with this.

"You mean we're going to gaslight the bastard? I'm totally on board with that."

"Step into the circle of protection, Anya. We have work to do," she said grimly.

They both seated themselves inside the witches' circle, created with chalk on the floor of the back room. The old book was between them. Once they began chanting, a slight breeze kicked up even though there were no windows in the room.

∞

"I feel a disturbance in the force." Ethan spoke in Anya's head in a teasing tone. "I warn you, Anya. Our bond is forever and I will destroy whoever is helping you."

Anya had just come home after spending most of the day casting the necessary spells with Catarina. Traffic had been hectic and she was definitely not in the mood for this bullshit. She reigned in her temper, thinking carefully before answering him. She had to stick to the plan no matter how much she wanted to cut him from chin to groin.

"How do you know that I'm Anya?" she said quietly. "What makes you think that I'm real? I could just be a voice that your sick mind manufactured."

She followed the plan perfectly and didn't answer as he spoke in her mind, his tone becoming more threatening by the second. She stayed quiet as he ranted and breathed a sigh of relief when the onslaught was over.

She picked up her cell phone. It was time to deal with Ethan Fallows exactly the way that Catarina had instructed.

∞

Ethan was sitting in one of the swings at the park when Anya arrived. The night sky was velvet black with a blanket of bright stars and Anya wondered why this couldn't be just any other ordinary night. The moon cast its bright light on the park, but for some reason, it looked ominous. She crossed her fingers, wishing all the bad luck in the world on Ethan.

As Anya approached the swings, Ethan looked up. She smiled brightly and enjoyed the look of confusion on his stupid face. She sat next to him on another swing, digging her tennis shoes into the sand.

"I'm glad you came," she said, maintaining the smile on her face.

"It's good to see you, Anya," Ethan said cautiously. He spoke in her mind. "I thought you would be spending most of your time at home, on your meds. What the hell are you up to?"

Anya appeared completely unaffected, never once showing how truly terrified she was. She answered in his head after a few long, tense moments.

"I'm not real, Ethan. I'm just one of the many voices that you made up in your head." She continued, speaking aloud. "Yeah, it's been a while since we've been here at our park. I'm sorry that I haven't been the best friend since I got sick months ago. We haven't written stories together in ages. I miss that."

They sat on the swings side by side for a long time, discussing a few of the many good times that they had shared. Anya could tell his guard was up, his laughter forced. She could tell that reminding him who he used to be and what he had become upset him. For a few moments during their long conversation, he became the old Ethan again. She came to the realization that she missed him and hated him at the same time.

Anya immediately strengthened her resolve to end this by whatever means necessary. He had declared war on her for whatever sick reasons, but he would find out soon that she was not one to just roll over and let things go. In fact, she had discovered just how vindictive she could be under the right circumstances.

"The demons are coming for you, Ethan. Just a friendly warning," she whispered in his mind. Her cheerful smile stayed in place. "It's getting late and I'd better head home," she said aloud.

They hugged awkwardly and said their goodbyes. Anya felt like running the entire distance to her car, but she maintained a leisurely walking pace. At the edge of the parking lot, she finally turned around. Ethan was walking away from the swings in the opposite direction. Anya laughed in his head. "You think you're actually hearing Anya in your head? No, you're just losing your mind. You just saw her and she's perfectly fine. You're the only one hearing voices."

Anya reached her Honda in the parking lot, got in, and sped off. She couldn't stop smiling.

∞

"Okay, all we need to do is complete the last spell," Catarina said to Anya as they sat in the witches' circle in the back room of Aware the next day. They were both dressed for comfort in old jeans and t-shirts. The pair had been working on the spells to stop Ethan since early that afternoon.

Anya watched Catarina sprinkle some sort of fragrant powder in the middle of the circle. "I could tell that he was confused and unsure of his actions last night. I think the gaslighting worked."

Catarina smiled a little and took both of Anya's hands in her own.

"Just wait until this whole summoning demons thing backfires on him," she reassured Anya. "There's going to be so much tripwire in his head that he won't be able to think coherently for years to come, quite possibly for the rest of his life."

"Great. Let's do this," Anya said with determination and no small amount of trepidation.

A few moments into the spell casting, a strong wind kicked up and blew out some of the candles. Catarina and Anya continued their task, undaunted by the spiritual forces now at work.

∞

Ethan couldn't recall when the demonic voices assailed him. He was at home now, upstairs in his room, studying a book about the occult. Perfecting his craft as a spell caster had become his top priority, aside from mind bonding with Anya. He had a sinking feeling that this mental attack was somehow connected to an unknown presence in Anya's life. She had never believed in the power of the occult and, therefore, couldn't be doing this to him without help.

"It's time to pay the price," a menacing voice said in his mind. Ethan clutched his head as the voices became louder, and he stood up from his desk.

"You promised to deliver the girl. You did not, so now you must pay up," another growling voice said.

For the first time, he felt real fear. He thought that he could control the demons and keep them doing his bidding. Now, they were demanding the payment he had promised but couldn't deliver on. His mind was consumed by a great number of demons, whispering foul things about what was waiting for him.

Ethan squeezed his head, willing the voices to go away.

"I'll give you the girl. I promise! I just need more time," he told the demons that he was sure were standing in his bedroom. He snatched up his pocket knife and sliced his palm, as he had done so many times before.

A demon laughed in his head. "Your blood is worthless to us."

Ethan dropped the knife, squeezed his temples, and screamed.

∞

One Month Later....

"Are you ready for this, Anya?" Catarina asked her friend as they approached the room in the psychiatric ward of the hospital.

"I'm more than ready. Hard to believe that I was a guest here months ago. Ethan did that to me. I don't feel a need to see his face ever again after today," Anya said, her face pensive. "His doctor said that he is now considered a long-term patient and that's damn good enough for me."

Anya slid the little window back and peered in on her fallen enemy. She was fine now, no voices, but the emotional scars of her captivity may never heal. Ethan sat in a corner of the room, his lips slack and chapped. His hair was unkempt and his skin was pale. He stared straight forward with glassy eyes, never moving.

Anya stepped aside and let Catarina see the damage. They looked in on him for a few more moments before Anya nodded. "Let's go. I'm satisfied."

The two young women shared a brief embrace before walking down the hospital corridor and out into the bright sunshine.

"I have a date tonight," Anya said as she and Catarina walked back to her Honda. "Really hot guy."

"Do you want me to cast a love spell?" Catarina asked, teasing.

Anya gave her a look. The last thing that she needed was another Ethan situation. "Hell no!" she said emphatically. She laughed, happy to be free.

∞

Ethan's eyes never moved, but his brain was working overtime. Each memory was like a land mine with a demon waiting to comment on it. There were so many voices filling his head. In his mind, he pictured slashing his palm with the pocket knife. When he was free – oh, he would be free someday – there would be hell to pay for certain parties. He smiled a little as he stared straight ahead, knowing his descent into madness had just begun.

Ex-Girlfriend

If you pester them enough, everyone has a story to tell. Some people's stories are riveting, while others' are only good enough for passing conversation. I'm standing here on a deserted road on a cold night, wondering how something so beautiful could go so incredibly wrong. My name is Christian Castro, and this is the story of how I lost it all.

∞

Meet Virginia. We all call her Ginni, and she was my girlfriend all through high school and into college. We were both completing our last year at a local community college in a small town named Caddo in Northern California. I'm a math major and Ginni studied English. She and I have lived in Caddo all of our lives, but we never met until high school. It was a heady combination of love and lust from the moment we made eye contact.

Ginni is small, with long dark hair, dark brown skin, and the most incredible big brown eyes I have ever seen. I have lighter skin, but it doesn't glow like hers. She has always loved my short, curly hair and she never seemed to go a whole day without telling me so.

Just last week, we were still in love and everything was great. I remember the last time that Ginni and I were happy together so clearly. We were walking through the Crossroads Mall, holding hands and stopping to kiss occasionally.

"Christian! OMG! There's a new tarot shop here," Ginni exclaimed excitedly. "Let's do it. Let's get a reading."

I rolled my eyes and laughed. "A tarot reading? Really? Ginni, how throwback era is that?"

She smiled and began pulling me toward the little shop. "Come on. You know you secretly want to!" She kissed my cheek and I caught a whiff of her expensive perfume. I was done

33

for, at that point. I was her willing slave. Anything Ginni Taylor wanted, I would give her.

We entered the shop and I was pleasantly surprised to see a young woman with dark hair, maybe a few years older than us, dressed neatly in jeans and a plain t-shirt. I guess I expected the whole Madame Zelda routine with the long skirt and scarf. She smiled in welcome.

"Hello. I'm Catarina. Would you like a tarot card reading?"

"Hi, Catarina. I'm Ginni and this is my boyfriend, Christian. We would *love* a reading."

Catarina invited us to have a seat and she prepared her cards. Everything was going fine and I found myself a little impressed by the woman's accuracy. It seemed like she'd known Ginni her whole life. Midway through the reading, Catarina turned over a card and her face froze.

"This card was… unexpected," the woman said. She moved her hand away and revealed it. It was the Death card. Ginni's smile faded and my heart began beating faster. I'm not a believer in fortune telling and all that other crap, but just seeing that card made my skin crawl.

Catarina visibly composed herself and put on a bright smile.

"The Death card is not always a bad sign. It can also represent a big change in your life, Ginni. I see a tremendous change in yours very soon."

We finished the tarot reading and left the shop, even though Ginni wanted to linger there. Her mood became bright again as I drove her home. We talked about things that made us laugh, both of us deliberately forgetting about that ominous Death card.

I dropped Ginni off at her house and she took her time getting out of my old Ford truck.

"Christian, I would never leave you," she said, kissing me gently. "You have my heart and you understand me when other people don't. I love that about you."

I watched her walk up the porch stairs and waved goodbye as she entered the house. I was riding on a love high all the way home. Those few words from her had further cemented my devotion. The only downer was the pile of homework that waited for me on my desk. I worked for a few hours, completing as many class assignments as possible. I didn't have class until well into the afternoon the next day, so I decided to go back to Ginni's place.

I drove as fast as always, taking the back streets. I rolled down the windows and felt the power of my big truck humming. The wind caught my hair and lifted it and I was elated. I pulled up across the street from Ginni's house and cut the engine. I saw a huge black motorcycle with a rider dressed in all black leather. My heart dropped in my chest when I saw Ginni embracing the man. I couldn't see his face clearly. I felt my hands shake in anger and jealousy. Ginni apparently didn't see me, but the rider did. He turned and looked directly at me and that stare will be with me forever. His eyes were bright orange flames. I dismissed that thought immediately, blaming it on my mind playing tricks.

∞

After that night, things between Ginni and I went downhill rather swiftly. She refused to take my calls and ignored my texts. She became distant and cold. The time we did spend together was brief and filled with arguments. And every night when I drove by her place, I saw the black leather rider. I finally told her that I knew she was cheating and demanded an explanation.

She shrugged indifferently and said, "You don't own me."

After I dropped her off, tears filling my eyes, I turned on the radio in my truck, hoping to catch some old rock song that would capture my dark mood. The first song that came on was a song about a girl who didn't want to be 'owned' by anyone. A chill ran down my spine.

∞

I shouldn't have been stalking my ex-girlfriend, but I couldn't help it. Tonight, I followed the black rider and Ginni as they rode away on his motorcycle. I thought about what a laugh my class attendance had become because of this catastrophic situation.

"Christian's the fool," I sang to myself, fighting back tears as I drove the Ford down the back streets of town, trying to keep up with the motorcycle. Just as I went to turn the radio up, I heard a deep voice in my mind.

"She's mine. She can't come back to you."

My heart stopped in my chest for a few moments.

∞

We're all standing here on this dirt road about 10 miles outside of Caddo and my heart is breaking. Looking in Ginni's eyes as she clings to the black rider, I know I've lost her and she's gone for good. I had caught up with them a few minutes before when they came to a stop in the middle of the road. I knew that they were waiting for me.

I pulled my truck alongside the motorcycle and jumped out. I immediately grabbed Ginni's arm to pull her to me but she backed away, snatching her arm from my hand. She clung to the dark rider.

"Christian, it's over. Let me go," Ginni said softly.

"What the hell, Ginni?" I demanded. "Maybe you don't belong with me anymore, but you don't belong with this guy, either. He looks dangerous. I worry about you. Hell, I still love you."

The black rider laughed from beneath his helmet and lifted it from his head. I felt my stomach turn. Those orange flame eyes were real. His dark skin seemed to glimmer in the moonlight and he sneered.

"Then you're a fool," he said curtly.

I took an unsteady breath.

"What... what are you?" I asked in shock.

"He's a death rider, Christian. And now, so am I. That's what the Death card meant for me," Ginni explained, her big eyes lighting up with orange flame. "He came for me, and now I have to go with him."

"What exactly is a death rider?" I asked, my voice trembling.

Ginni's smile was nothing pleasant.

"We reap souls when it's their time." She cocked her head to the side. Her long, dark hair was like a beautiful waterfall spilling over her shoulders. I suddenly remembered all the times I had caressed the silken strands. "That's all I'll say about that."

She moved away from the death rider and took my face in her hands.

"I don't have the capacity for human love anymore, but I'll remember you, Christian. And, when it's your time to go, I'll be the one to hold you. I promise I'll make your final ride unforgettable."

"Let's ride," the death rider said shortly. He put on his helmet and straddled the motorcycle.

I stared into the flames in her eyes, searching for something – anything – left of my Ginni. She jumped on the back of the death rider's motorcycle and turned around. She winked at me before patting the rider on the shoulder. They took off at great speed and she never looked back.

∞

Well, this is the part where I introduced myself and told you my story. I could tell you that my heart is shattered and I may never love again. Love is karmic, though. I see that now. The love I gave will be returned to me one day.

I looked at my truck and then up at the moon and stars. I thought about how trivial so many things in my life seemed now. I thought about my final ride into eternity, hopefully many years from now. I knew I'd see Ginni again with certainty. I thought about how I'd curse her out for abandoning me.

I walked back toward my Ford and I began to laugh... and I couldn't stop.

A Little Blood Between Friends

"Oh, hurry the hell up," Delilah muttered under her breath, kneading the small black knit bag with nervous hands. She glanced around the place, a bar named Vivian's in a not-so-great area of downtown Los Angeles, taking in the dim lighting and scuffed hardwood floors. She'd been waiting here for what seemed like hours for an acquaintance of her younger brother, Declan.

She didn't even know why she was here. No, she corrected herself. She was here because she couldn't say no to Declan whenever he got himself between a rock and hard place, which was often. *There's no way in hell I want to be here too late into the evening,* she thought as the bar's main door opened, letting in a rowdy bunch of people. She could see that it was well beyond dusk.

∞

He came in unobtrusively right behind the raucous crowd of people who had just entered the bar. His way was to enter a scene quietly, keeping to the shadows of a room. His close clipped black hair, arresting blue green eyes, and pale skin served to make sure he didn't stay unnoticed for long. He had to make this quick.

He saw her right away, the sister. The resemblance between Declan McDade and his sister, the lovely Delilah, was marked. They shared the same dark hair and olive skin. She was twisting long brown strands of her hair around two fingers and looking around anxiously. He grinned darkly. Declan had become an annoyance and he had little patience for him. Well, he wouldn't keep her waiting. He headed in her direction.

∞

This has to be Ash Lockler, Delilah thought, almost knocking over her water glass as a powerfully built man with cropped black hair approached her table. She noted his jeans and black leather jacket. He looked... tough.

"Ash Lockler?" Delilah said, looking up at him.

Ash nodded and neatly folded his big frame into the booth's bench seat opposite her. He didn't smile, but then she hadn't really expected him to. This was a simple business transaction for Declan and there was no time for exchanging pleasantries.

"I trust you'll provide what I expect," Ash asked quietly, taking in her pretty face framed by all that long dark hair. She would do nicely.

Delilah hesitated, meeting his eyes. He was really a breathtaking man and those eyes were to die for. She caught herself staring and grabbed her small bag, reaching inside.

"Yes. I have it right here. Five thousand cash. You can count it. That should settle my brother's debt to you."

Ash's eyes narrowed in irritation. Declan McDade. The little weasel. His next words were measured.

"Delilah, I'm afraid that five thousand doesn't even come close to what your brother owes me. His debt is a lot closer to one hundred thousand dollars."

Delilah felt her lips go slack with shock and she promptly snapped her mouth shut. Ash went on.

"Your money, in short, is no good. A different sort of... payment was arranged between me and Declan."

"What do you want, then? My house?" Delilah's voice was strangely hoarse and she took a hasty sip of water.

"No, your house is safe. I want your body," Ash replied simply.

The water came flying out of her mouth before she could stop it.

"I'm sorry, did you just say you want my *body*?" A wave of anger filled her instantly. She knew exactly what the man had said. Damn Declan!

Ash nodded and watched the many emotions play across her face. He knew she was blazingly angry. You didn't live as long as he had without knowing a little something about how human emotions work. Surprisingly, the remaining water in her glass didn't splash in his face.

"It's not that kind of party, Mr. Lockler," Delilah said, her tone frosty. She grabbed her little black bag and left the booth, heading for the main door of the bar. She was mortified and sincerely hoped that no one in this dive bar had overheard her strange conversation.

Ash sighed, rubbing the bridge of his nose in aggravation. Declan McDade had caused him much inconvenience for quite some time. Maybe it was time for him to just be dead and he wouldn't have to deal with this shit anymore. He watched Delilah's hips sway in her grey sweater dress and black heels as she exited the bar, and he moved quickly to catch up to her.

Delilah was halfway across the crowded parking lot before she felt a strong hand grip her arm. She turned around, knowing full well that some people couldn't let things go and take no for a simple answer.

"Get off me!"

"Declan will pay that debt one way or the other, Delilah," Ash said coldly.

"Are you threatening us? I offered you five thousand dollars, but my body is not for settling debts. Take what I have and leave us alone."

Ash hated the thought of glamouring, her but his body was starving. He caught her arms, pulling her roughly to him. He smiled and caught her big brown eyes with his.

"I'm not going to hurt you and you have no reason to fear or reject me. In fact, I can have you in your home, in the back seat of your car, or up against the wall in the alley. Your choice." He had no intention of having sex with her, of course. He had plenty of other willing female vampires for that. This was all about his blood lust.

Delilah felt like she was drowning in Ash's eyes. Her knees were weak and she heard his words from a distance. Her whole being was focused on his amazing eyes and the cadence of his words. She nodded in acquiescence.

"We can go to my home." She paused, licking her lips. "Ash, are we friends?" she asked suddenly.

Ash gave her a reassuring smile. "Yes, Delilah, we're old friends. I'll drive."

∞

"So many vampire books," Ash murmured, scanning Delilah's crammed bookshelves. There was a small collection of romance novels and thrillers, but there were far more books about vampires. They were in her house now, a modest beige townhouse in Pasadena not far from the Rose Bowl. On arriving, she had invited him in without giving it a second thought. Of course, she was still under the mistaken belief that they were old friends. On the drive over, he had concocted an entire history of their friendship, including a friendship with her brother.

Delilah smiled, coming to stand next to Ash and holding a glass of red wine. "Vampires are a passion of mine. I thought you knew that about me." Her tone was questioning.

"I was just remarking that there seem to be even more vampire books than the last time I was here," Ash replied smoothly. He picked a book from one of the shelves and read the title aloud. *"Blood Lust of the Damned."* He snorted. "How appropriate." His thirst for her blood wasn't easily controlled, but he was managing it for the moment.

Delilah felt like she was swimming in a fathomless deep. Her thoughts were disjointed and she couldn't seem to focus on one particular notion for very long. She knew that she and Ash had been friends for many years, yet there was a burgeoning attraction to him. As he continued to examine her books, her mind conjured up images of his pale skin next to her darker skin as he kissed her.

"Would you like a glass of wine?" She moved away from him, out of his disturbing orbit. It was becoming difficult to concentrate. There was something, a logical train of thought she had been following that she couldn't remember. *Why is Ash so pale and cold?* her mind whispered.

"No, thank you," Ash responded, his tone distracted. He watched her sit and his eyes were drawn to the contrast of her dark hair and dress against the deep crimson of her sofa. Delilah McDade was an enchanting little thing and snippy as hell when she wasn't glamoured. Her home was also a pleasant surprise, done in crimson and black. The colors spoke to him, his own expensive loft in downtown Los Angeles decorated completely in black.

"Have a seat, Ash. Your flight to Denver doesn't leave for a few hours." He came to sit on a red chair directly across from her and Delilah smiled warmly. She felt flirty tonight. Ash always made her feel crazy attractive and wildly flirtatious. "Are you pale all over?"

"I don't like the sun much."

"Are those contact lenses?"

"All me."

"Why are you so cold? I mean, your skin is practically subzero."

"Low blood pressure."

"Will you kiss me?"

Ash hesitated before answering. "As much as I'd really like to, I'm going to say no. Your brother wouldn't appreciate one of his oldest friends hitting on his sister."

Delilah moved without a word and stood directly in front of him. "I'm going to sit in your lap, Ash, and you're going to tell me exactly why we shouldn't be more than friends." She sat, straddling his legs and wrapping her arms around his big shoulders. "I've known you forever. Isn't this the next logical step?"

Ash's eyes narrowed thoughtfully. This was a perfect position to simply take what he needed. Very soon, he would be caught up in bloodlust as he nearly was back in the parking lot earlier. He smiled at Delilah disarmingly, first stroking her dark hair then trailing his fingers down her neck. He genuinely liked her. Remarkably, even though he had only known her for a couple of hours, she was becoming more than just a blood bag to him. He would take what he needed and not a drop more. He kissed her neck and she moaned softly in his ear.

He's so cold, Delilah thought, thoroughly enjoying his soft, cool lips doing incredible things to her. His extraordinary eyes flashed into her mind and a whisper of her earlier train of thought returned. Could it be...? Impulsively, she pulled away from him, seeing his confusion. She slapped him. Hard. His fangs ran out immediately and he growled menacingly low in this throat. He grabbed her shoulders roughly.

Delilah gasped in wonder, reaching up to stroke one of his fangs gently. "Vampire," she said in breathless delight. "You *are* real."

Ash swore under his breath and instantly began damage control.

"Delilah, this is nothing new. You've always known that I was a vampire and that's the main reason that we haven't been and cannot be together physically. I would probably really hurt you in bed."

She frowned in confusion. Her mind was so fuzzy but her heart was so full she was sure that she would explode. Ash was a real vampire and he was her old friend. "I've always known? Does Declan know?"

"No, this secret is strictly between you and me. You must keep quiet about it."

"Are there many more of you? Tell me everything!" Delilah bounced around in his lap with joyful abandon and he felt his body respond. He was fighting a losing battle.

"You already know everything about me. You just have to remember." His voice was gently chiding.

"Well, you'll have to tell me again," she demanded playfully.

Ash's voice was soft and thoughtful as he told her stories of his past, careful to leave out names and specific details. She hung on every word and he caught glimpses of the child she had been. He knew that she was in her early thirties, with Declan five years behind her. He could easily picture what she would look

44

like as an old woman. And, where would he be? Somewhere still under the thumb of the Vampire Council and still trying to come to grips with what he was.

"Tell me more about your past before you became a bad-ass vamp," Delilah said eagerly. She still sat straddling him.

Ash's lip tilted up slightly at the pet name she had for his kind. She was glamoured and likely wouldn't remember any of this, so he felt safe confiding in her.

"I was born Asher John Lockler in 1912 in a small town called Caddo, far up in Northern California. That little town has prospered and is still around today, although I won't dare go back in the foreseeable future. I can't risk being recognized. I'm an only child. My parents are buried there. I was turned by my maker when I was 20." He sighed. "Enough talk." He pulled her close and nuzzled her neck.

"Oh, do you need to feed?" Delilah tilted her head back, exposing her throat.

"You would let me... feed from you?"

"Of course. What's a little blood between friends?" she quipped. He laughed.

Curiosity struck him and he pulled back a little.

"What do you do for a living now, Delilah?" He watched the fleeting trace of disappointment on her face and laughed inwardly. So eager to be so close to death. He didn't lie to himself. He knew what he was. A little more information about her was all he wanted. His thirst was nearly raging, but he found that he needed to satisfy his intense desire to know more about her before taking her blood. She was a blood donor to settle a debt and nothing more, he reminded himself.

"I'm still a toy design consultant for Kinder Fun," Delilah said. At his blank look, she explained more in detail. "Know that child's game, Bouncin' Blocks? All my work. I created that." She sounded proud of her accomplishment.

Ash nodded in understanding. "Sounds like you're doing well for yourself." He looked around her place again, cataloging every book, rug, and throw pillow.

"After six years at the university earning both of my degrees, I expect nothing less," she replied. She leaned forward to be closer to him, leaning her head on his shoulder. He stroked her hair and she sighed in contentment.

"I take it that a husband and the birth of children will be next for you?" he asked softly, trailing his fingers down her spine. She shivered a bit at his touch.

"Soon, but not now. There's quite a lot that I want to do with my life. Then there's Declan to take care of...." Her voice trailed off.

The thought of Declan taking advantage of her, even in small ways, pissed him off a little. He had quickly offered up his sister as a sex partner to settle a huge debt and probably expected Delilah to comply. He was nothing more than a low-lying snake in high grass, as far as Ash was concerned. He would glamour him later.

"Parenthood is a joy that I will probably never experience. I envy you."

"So, vamps can't make babies?" Delilah said slowly.

He shrugged. "I've never tried, but it has happened. I suppose if my body temperature was ever warm enough my seed could produce a child. Highly improbable, though."

His pensive look spoke volumes to her and she caressed his face gently. He kissed the palm of her hand, eyes closed. She planted little kisses on his neck, trying to make him feel as good as he had made her feel. Ash withstood the sweet torment before his control broke and he kissed her roughly.

They sat in her chair as she straddled him, kissing for long moments. The moment his tongue met hers, she was done for. She so wanted this vampire to touch her everywhere, to take her. Her thoughts were still in a jumble, but this made perfect sense in the snowstorm of madness in her head.

Ash quickly unbuttoned the top of her sweater dress, impatiently pushing it down around her waist. Her bra was black lace and he took a moment to appreciate it before unclasping the front, baring her breasts. Shame he would never see the panties.

46

"This will hurt," he said softly, sinking his fangs into the side of one lovely breast. She gasped in shock.

Delilah felt herself sinking into the sweetest maelstrom ever. His lips drawing blood from her was better than the best sex she had ever had. She cupped his head in her hands, murmuring encouraging words. He continued until she told him that she was dizzy. He retracted his fangs and pulled back to look at her, his lips stained with her blood.

"That was unforgettable. Really intense," Delilah said, fighting to stay awake. Her eyelids kept closing and the room was spinning. She rested her head on his shoulder as he closed her bra and dress, placing her on the sofa. She quickly dropped off to sleep.

He leaned over and kissed her forehead. He didn't dare linger there. His thirst had been quenched and now she had aroused another great need. He would find another willing blood donor and sex partner. Delilah deserved far better than this. The debt was paid in full. He thought about glamouring her again to erase her memories of him and this night. He decided to leave things as they were. If she did have brief snatches of memory, hopefully she would recall meeting her first vampire with childlike joy. He wanted her to remember the one hot night with a vampire that he had given her until she was an old woman.

Ash left her sleeping and opened her front door. Back to his real life as an undead, such as it was. He was still very much owned by the Vampire Council and one didn't ignore a summons from them. There was no place in his life for tender things.

"Good night, Delilah," Ash whispered. He closed her front door.

Thea's Mirror

"Triple Threat, please, Andy," Thea said softly to the bartender, smiling. She sat comfortably on a bar stool in the Dollhouse, a bar in downtown Pasadena, not far from her modest apartment. She was teetering on the edge of drunk and all was right in her world. *It's really too bad that I need alcohol to make my problems seem less daunting,* she thought.

Thea twirled a short brown strand of hair around her fingers as she waited for her last drink of the night. She caught a glimpse of herself in the huge antique mirror hanging above the bar. Her lips curled up in a smile. The mirror had belonged to her grandmother, Virgie, and she had left it to her along with a small amount of money and the rest of her meager possessions. In life, Virgie hadn't been anywhere near wealthy, but she had been happy. Thea, feeling philanthropic, had donated the expensive mirror to the Dollhouse a few years ago.

"Here you go, Thea," Andy said, sliding the drink across the bar to her. She thanked him and took a few sips. With a sidelong glance, he noted the dark circles under her eyes. Thea had been a regular in the bar for the past few years and they had established an easy, casual friendship. She was a truly pretty woman, with dark hair and a curvy figure. He hated to see her look so tired and beaten by life.

Thea swiveled on the bar stool, facing the crowd. She perused tonight's throng of patrons and thought briefly about doing something as daring as taking one of these available men home because she knew she was emotionally unavailable and could use some no-strings sex. She dismissed the idea just as quickly. She hadn't descended that far into desperation, thank God.

She just needed to finish this drink and be alone tonight, like so many other nights since her life had ended.

∞

Thea congratulated herself on not stumbling on her way out of the front door of the bar. She walked slowly to the curb to hail a cab, enjoying the effect of her mild buzz. The warmth seemed to start in her stomach and radiated all the way to her fingertips and toes. A light rain had begun to fall and she pulled her mini-umbrella from the pocket of her black peacoat and covered herself. The night sky was dark and ominous, but this was her favorite sort of weather.

"But it *never* rains in Southern California," Thea murmured to herself, laughing a little.

She stood by the curb for several minutes before a cab finally pulled over. When she got inside, the pervasive warmth of the car's heater spread all over her body, nauseating her slightly.

She gave the cab driver her home address in South Pasadena. She prided herself on being a responsible drinker, never driving after drinking. She laid her head back against the headrest and closed her eyes. Suddenly, Virgie's rose garden came to mind. Maybe it was time to call her mom and mend the fences after their last spectacular blowout argument. She debated whether or not to call her mother, Emma. She reflected on her life so far as the cab sped toward its destination.

∞

Thea was in her early thirties, unmarried and childless at this point. She only had one person left alive in her life and that was Emma. Thea was an only child and had a nagging feeling of loss for siblings that never were. She'd only had two serious romantic relationships in her life, and one of those boyfriends was dead.

Brian. She hadn't thought of him in months and he had been in the ground for close to ten years. A month after college graduation, he had picked up a gun and blown a hole in his head. She remembered his tall, lean build, dark hair, and brown eyes always filled with some kind of mischief.

Presently, Thea was a first grade elementary school teacher in the local district where she herself had attended school, and she sincerely loved her career. Great job, great friends, so-so family life. What could be wrong? Still, she felt like something was missing.

∞

Later that night as the rain fell, Thea dreamed that she was dressed in a white flannel nightgown, one of Virgie's, and she was walking on broken glass from a mirror. Her feet throbbed and bled, but she just kept walking back and forth on the glass. In the dream, her location changed and she suddenly found herself in Virgie's rose garden and her grandmother sat on the porch. Virgie put a finger to her own lips in a shushing motion. Thea was trapped among the roses. She looked closer. The roses were covered in blood.

She woke up shivering.

∞

"But what if the monster gets me when I get on the bus?"

Thea's answering smile was both warm and tired.

"Julian, the monster won't get you today. It never does. Remember, we locked it inside of the classroom closet."

"What if someone let it out by mistake? It could have eaten them and then come looking for me," Julian reasoned with his six year old logic.

Thea touched the top of his blond hair reassuringly.

"I won't let him get you. I promise. Now let's get you on the school bus before it leaves without you."

After Thea had done her duty for the day, she realized that she was bordering on exhaustion. As she packed up her teacher carrier, she couldn't stop yawning and her eyelids felt gritty. The nightmare had interrupted her sleep last night, so perhaps a nap was in order. This was the beginning of her weekend, so she could pretty much do what she wanted.

∞

In her dream, Thea was cautiously walking though Virgie's rose garden again, glancing at the vibrant roses dripping blood. She looked up to find her grandmother seated in her favorite white wicker chair, humming softly.

"Careful, child. There are snakes in the high grass."

"Grammy Virgie?" Thea questioned in wonder. She searched the area near her feet. "I don't see any snakes."

"Not all snakes are easily seen. For some, you have to know how to find them and get away quick," Virgie explained softly. "There isn't much time, so I'll be quick. Bad things are coming. Whatever you do, don't invite hell on earth. Don't touch that mirror when you see something in it you shouldn't be seeing."

Thea shook her head in confusion. "The big antique? Your mirror?"

"That mirror is a doorway to all other mirrors, which can be a passage from your world to mine. It always has been since I blessed it years ago."

"Blessed it?" Thea thought for a moment before comprehension dawned. "Grammy, were you a witch?"

Virgie smiled gently. "From birth. The magic skipped a generation and was gifted to you instead." She scowled. "Which is good because Emma couldn't pull her head out of a potato sack, let alone do some serious magic."

"I have magic powers?" Thea said, dumbfounded. "I can cast spells and all that?"

Virgie gave her a sobering look. "And you're going to need all of your power and strength to resist or defeat what's coming. Guard yourself against the snake, child. That's all I can tell you now." She put a finger to her lips in the same shushing motion.

Thea woke up from her nap a little after midnight, the witching hour.

∞

The vivid dreams about Grammy Virgie haunted Thea all day. They troubled her so much that she drank significantly less that evening. The regular crowd was there, plus a few more. Andy had just served her a drink and she found her eyes drawn to the old mirror. She wished that she could better recall what Grammy had been trying to tell her.

Suddenly, something moved inside the mirror. She turned around quickly to see what had caused the strange ripple effect. She found nothing, but when she turned to face the mirror again she saw a familiar face. Thea almost dropped her drink as a very dead Brian walked from the shadows and ripples of the old mirror to touch the glass from his side. He was completely naked. She noted, half hysterically, that he looked remarkably good for a dead man.

"Touch my hand, Thea. Get me out of here. This place is God-awful boring." She realized that he had whispered in her mind. She was up and in front of the mirror like a shot, driven to know if this was an alcohol-induced hallucination. She remembered her grandmother's admonition about the mirror but chose to ignore it. What harm could come to her? Besides, if she wasn't crazy drunk she was seeing a man long dead who had chosen to visit her.

Thea touched the mirror with careful fingers, as if she would be burned. Brian smiled at her before disappearing, leaving a series of strong ripples in the glass. She felt a sharp pang of disappointment that this was probably just a creation of her mind. She went back to her barstool dejectedly and finished her drink.

∞

Thea awoke to the sound of glass shattering. She sat up in bed abruptly and searched the dark bedroom for a moment before turning on her lamp on the nightstand. She drew in a sharp breath and made little panting cries. There was a bleeding naked man on her floor curled into a fetal position and breathing heavily. He looked up. *Brian,* she thought in shock. Brian had apparently crawled through her big bedroom mirror and splintered it in the process. *Come from where?* a tiny voice whispered in her mind.

Brian gave Thea a wry smile and she finally understood what they say about how people never change. Thea immediately walked over to where he was on the carpeted floor, trying to avoid the glass shards. She touched his face, feeling muscle and bone. More of Grammy Virgie's dreams were coming back to her, but she still felt like she was missing something important.

"My God, Brian, you're dead! You can't be here. You just can't...."

"I needed to talk to you, Thea." He gave her a considering look. "You look like hell. Not what I expected to find."

"I didn't expect to find a dead man in my bedroom tonight. Did you fake your death?"

Brian sat up as much as he could and shook his head. His face twisted as if he was dealing with some hidden anguish.

"No," he finally replied. "I wish it was that simple. I was as dead as they come."

"Where have you been? Where did you come from just now?"

"A place of shadows and things that go bump. Been waiting a while for you to get me out of there," he spoke calmly. "Hey, can I have a robe?"

All the world had stopped tonight, leaving only her swiftly beating heart and the promise that she had been chosen to experience something miraculous.

∞

"I can't believe that you were suffering all this time, Brian," Thea said quietly, unable to stop staring at the man who had meant so much to her. Just over an hour ago, her very dead ex had come crashing through her bedroom mirror, completely naked, from a hellish place of torment. He was now wearing one of her old plush white robes as he sat across from her in a big comfy chair in her living room. He reached over and ran his fingers through her short dark hair. Thea held his hand in one of hers for a moment, then let go. He sat back in the chair.

Brian nodded, his face somber.

"Committing suicide seemed like an easy way out all those years ago. But I never thought that God would turn His back on me for one thoughtless mistake." He paused, meeting Thea's eyes. He pushed a lock of his dark hair away from his face. "And I want you to know that my actions were pretty thoughtless, Thea. I didn't think about you or my family when I blasted myself. I was under too much pressure and couldn't handle it."

"How did you get free from... where you were?" Thea was hesitant in her phrasing.

Brian shook his head and his expression was sorrowful. "But I'm not free. Not really. I can only be back here for a couple of days, at most. I just came back to say goodbye to you properly. If you don't mind, I want to spend my brief time being with you. I want to you to have good memories of me. I came back for you more than any other reason."

They spent the next hour discussing the afterlife and what its existence meant. Thea had moments of doubt like anyone else when it came to heaven and hell, but she considered herself to still be a good woman and a sometimes practicing Methodist. Brian's descriptions of the place of shadows were so vivid that tears formed in her eyes. God wouldn't do this. There had to be some kind of mistake.

When the discussion ended, Thea went to the hall closet and loaded her arms with fresh linens and pillows. She put them down on the sofa and turned to look at him.

"I hope you're comfortable sleeping here." She felt a bit self-conscious under his piercing gaze. She denied the thought as it came to her, but she was also wary, for some reason. Something was off and she wondered if it had anything to do with Grammy Virgie's warning.

"If you don't want me here, I'll understand. I hate to think that you're letting me stay with you because of some misguided sense of loyalty to a dead ex."

Thea's smile was sleepy but genuine. "I wouldn't have you sleep anywhere else."

∞

Brian greeted her the next morning when she entered the living room, and she had to admit that she was pleased he was still around. She willed herself to remain emotionally detached from him because he would be gone again, this time probably for good. She decided to just be a friend to him.

"You're going to need more than a robe. Let's hit up Target today and get you some clothes," Thea suggested.

Brian gestured at the robe. "My naked body underneath this robe is keeping you from thinking clearly, right?"

Thea headed back to her bedroom to shower but gave him a cheeky smile over her shoulder.

"Uh-huh." She kicked herself mentally. *No flirting,* she told herself firmly.

Brian laughed and began folding the linen.

∞

Later that night, Thea began to dream. She was standing in the middle of Virgie's rose garden and, once again, the roses were dripping blood. She found herself suddenly looking for snakes in the high grass. She walked slowly through the garden, trying to avoid being scratched by the rose bushes. She wore the same flannel nightgown, which had been Virgie's. She didn't see her grandmother this time, but her voice was clear.

"That's better, child. You're looking for those snakes I was telling you about. You're gonna need help since you touched the old mirror even after I warned you not to," Virgie admonished. "A whole heap of trouble is heading your way, little Thea, and I need to help you defend yourself."

The scene changed and Thea found herself in the attic of the house she had grown up in. Emma, her mother, still lived there with any number of men whom she was sleeping with.

Emma played the part of the conservative well enough, but Thea had never been fooled.

"Why are we here, Grammy?" Thea asked, looking around.

"I made your mother promise to keep a few of my things here in this attic after I passed away. There are books and other important things here that you will need. See that trunk over there? That's another gift from me to you."

"What danger am I in?" Thea asked, a tiny sliver of fear traveling down her spine.

"Things are murky now, but your vision will soon clear and you will be able to see some things as they really are."

Thea shot up suddenly, gripping the pillow and crying out. She took a shuddering breath and tried to calm herself. The dream had been just as vivid and cryptic as the other ones, but she could remember this one from beginning to end. She glanced over at the clock, surprised that it was only a few minutes after midnight. It seemed like she'd been with her grandmother for hours. She hoped that her cry hadn't woken Brian, who slept soundly in the living room. She would definitely be taking a trip to her old attic tomorrow, and that meant spending time with her mother, Emma. She was only coming for the trunk and knew that her swift departure from the family home would make both of them happy.

∞

"I can't imagine what you would want with that dusty old thing," Emma said, shaking her head as Thea assessed the outside of the trunk. She didn't dare open it in front of her mother. She instinctively knew that Grammy Virgie wanted it that way.

"I'm leaving the trunk here with you, Mom, but I will be here in the attic often over the next few weeks. I promise I won't disturb you and your... guests," Thea said, looking up from the large black trunk.

"Good lord, can't you just take that dirty old thing with you?" Emma asked impatiently.

"I don't have room for it at my place." Thea sighed. She noted the new red highlights in her mother's dark hair. Her mom definitely had a sleepover guest on his way to the house.

Emma waved a careless hand.

"Fine, fine. I'll keep that piece of junk here. Even though you moved out, you, of course, are still welcome here any time." She turned and began heading down the stairs from the attic. "Just call first. Common courtesy."

Thea kneeled down and, with great effort, opened the old trunk. It was satin-lined and almost perfect inside. She pulled out a huge book of spells, a few vials of unidentified powders, a box of chalk, and a few white candles. She carefully set everything in front of her before turning her attention to the spell book.

She read for a whole hour before coming across an interesting spell in the book. The spell was a request to the universe to reveal a person's real emotions and true agenda. *This could be useful,* she thought with Brian in mind. She reached into her small handbag and grabbed the lighter she had brought with her for this situation. She carefully lit two of the candles and placed them in front of a large, old mirror in the corner of the attic.

Next, she drew a witch's circle with the chalk just as the book had instructed. She picked up the heavy book and set it down next her inside the circle. A dull hum began close to her ears and she had her first taste of real power as short bursts of energy surged up and down her arms. She began casting her first spell.

∞

Brian was reclined on Thea's sofa watching the television when the demon bounty hunter bent and warped the new long mirror in Thea's bedroom without shattering it and came through from the shadow place. He had no time for games from this pathetic soul. There was no escape from his master's domain. Ever.

Brian jumped up from the sofa fearfully when the hunter strode from the bedroom to the living room. He smiled and pointed at Brian.

"You have yet to deliver what you promised to us. You're not welshing on us, are you?"

Brian shook his head rapidly.

"I just need more time here, Ryu."

Ryu was all strong muscle, brawn and dark skin in human form. In demon form, he was even more terrifying. He was a bounty hunter from the hell dimension who had never lost a runaway soul.

"Bring the girl to me by midnight. One of you will cross the threshold into the hell regions tonight. Pray that it's not you."

∞

Thea saw every moment of the exchange between Brian and the demon in her mind's eye. She knew that this Ryu was anything but human. The spell she had cast revealed not only Brian's emotions and agenda, but it showed her Ryu's true face. She knew that the demon expected Brian to happily trade places with her and leave her tortured and suffering in the shadow place.

Righteous anger overtook her and her hands shook as the scene in her mind faded. Grammy Virgie, for her own reasons, hadn't shown her any of this. Maybe her precious grandmother had wanted her to come to her own realization that Brian was using her all along. She also accepted the fact that God definitely knew what he was doing when he left Brian to suffer for an eternity. She had no intention of going peacefully into the pits of hell. A plan was taking shape in her mind and she began searching the book.

∞

Thea had spent most of the day preparing for Brian's well-deserved send-off party for two. She had her short bob styled first thing in the morning. A pampering mani-pedi was next, then off to the mall for a new dress. When she made it back, she and Brian carefully moved the long mirror from her bedroom into the living room. Thea deliberately lit the thick white candles as dusk approached.

Brian couldn't stop staring at her, taking in the little black dress and flirty black heels. He complimented her as they sat on the sofa drinking wine after dinner. Thea had to admit that Brian was just plain hot in jeans and a button-down white shirt. *Too bad he's going back to hell,* she thought wryly.

Thea stood and extended her hand to Brian. "Let's dance," she said, flashing a bright smile. She had turned on the radio in the living room earlier, choosing a jazz and blues station. Brian had all the right moves, swaying with her to the music. She stealthily maneuvered him over to the mirror in the corner.

She was never sure which one of them kissed the other first. Brian's lips were baby soft and she wished, for a brief moment, that it didn't have to end this way. She had trusted him and look what it had gotten her. She had him perfectly positioned in front of the mirror, with his back to it.

She whispered a few words she had learned from the book of spells and the mirror began to ripple. She looked up at Brian, smiling serenely as if nothing had ever separated them.

"I love you, Brian. A part of me always will." She stroked his cheek with her fingers. "But, I love me more."

Thea shoved Brian toward the long mirror as hard as she could. He looked shocked as he stumbled backwards and fell into the ripples of the mirror. He was halfway between worlds. Ryu, the bounty hunter, was right there to catch his fall. He wrapped his huge arms around Brian's neck and pulled him all the way back to the shadow place.

"No, Thea! I love you and I came back just for you. Why have you done this?"

She could hear the sounds of torture and misery form the other side coupled with Ryu's mocking laughter. She couldn't tear her eyes away from the mirror until Brian and his captor disappeared from sight. The images of the shadow place faded and the mirror was just a mirror again.

"Good girl," Virgie whispered in her ear. "You just keep practicing your spells and you'll be fine."

Thea wasn't sure if she would ever see Grammy Virgie again in her dreams, but every time she passed a mirror, she was sure that she wouldn't just be checking her hair. She would be looking for quick glimpses of a particular rose garden tended to by a happy old woman who just wanted to be remembered.

Disturbia

"So, now you're Casey's chauffeur as well as her designated driver," Lucky McCall commented dryly to her friend, Daniel. "That's a step up. Before, you were just her beer flunky."

Daniel Hughes, a self-admitted doormat when it came to beautiful chicks, shot Lucky, his close friend of one year, a middle finger and laughed sheepishly.

"You know how hard it is to tell Casey no. She'll have a meltdown that will last at least a week." He paused thoughtfully. "Plus, the sex is so good."

Lucky rolled her eyes and tucked a few short dark brown strands of hair behind her ear. As he went on and on about the goddess Casey, she surveyed Daniel's longish blond hair and vibrant hazel eyes, his face animated with excitement and genuine affection for the worthless slut. Casey Clifton was wealthy, privileged, and clearly using Daniel. It was so obvious to everyone in their close-knit, middle class social circle, but Daniel didn't really seem to care about that part. His thoughts on the matter were pretty straightforward – he sure was using Casey, too. He waved a large hand in front of Lucky's field of vision.

"You still with me?" Daniel asked. He knew that Lucky absolutely could not stand Casey and the thought lifted his heart and stroked his ego. There was something between him and Lucky, something that sizzled, comforted, and dug in deep all at the same time. They'd been hanging with the same group a little more than a year now and he had grown close to Lucky. He liked and respected her beyond mere sexual attraction. Soon, he would have to have a little taste of her. Her luscious, full lips were curved in a smile as she waved back at him. Oh, crap. What had she been saying for the past few moments?

"Are you still with me?" Lucky asked slyly. She laughed a little as he struggled to recall her last few comments and was struck again by her beauty. Her bright teeth contrasted against her dark skin and her chin-length bob haircut framed an incredibly pretty face. She wore a black sundress and leather sandals. He thanked God every day that she was single. Lucky opened her small straw bag and took out a CD in a clear plastic case.

"Do you want more coffee?" she asked, standing but leaving the straw bag on the table. They were at one of their usual hangout spots, a small coffee house called Sacred Grounds. Daniel nodded and watched her turn away with their coffee cups in her hands and the CD tucked under her arm. "Trust me," she said over her shoulder. "This is one of my special mixtapes. You need this."

She was back at their table in a few minutes, setting down steaming cups of fresh coffee. The music began to blare from the strategically placed speakers on shelves in two corners of the coffee house, clearly alternative rock instead of the light jazz playing a moment ago. Lucky grinned.

"This is the new Matchbox Twenty. Track five of my mixtape. This is a song about a really mean girl and the guy who puts up with her nonsense." She reached over and smacked the back of Daniel's head before sitting down. "Wait until we get to Track nine. Maroon 5 has a good song that tells a similar story about a mean girl."

"Enough about Casey," he lamented playfully. "Next year, UC Berkeley!" They toasted each other with their cups of coffee. "Rancho Tehama is buzzing tonight. It's good to see people out there having fun in spite of the murders."

Lucky nodded. "The cops lifted the mandatory curfew while you were in Vegas with your dad last week. The press gave the killer his own moniker – the Baby Doll Killer. The media says that he started sending mangled baby dolls to the police. They say that the dolls are posed in the shoeboxes just like his victims at the murder scenes."

They talked about the gruesome murders that had begun earlier that summer in the small, Northern California town of Rancho Tehama, where their whole social crowd had grown up and now attended the cozy local community college. It was crazy to imagine that some local resident was possibly stabbing young women. They were both grateful that no one they knew had been killed.

"There you are, D-Bear!" Casey said loudly, interrupting their conversation as she approached the table. Casey Clifton was hell on heels in high wedged sandals, a snug tank top, and cut off shorts. "I have been texting you like crazy for the past hour. Have the decency to answer when I do that." She lifted her long, auburn ponytail and draped it across one shoulder with a beguiling smile. "Lucky," she acknowledged her with a nod.

Lucky pasted on a bright, fake smile. "Casey."

Daniel took one last gulp of coffee and stood from the table.

"I have to cancel the movie tonight," he said. "I had my cell on silent and I just forgot to call you, Casey. My old man has a long list of chores for me and I'd better get started this afternoon. Plus, I'm not really dressed properly." He gestured at his jeans and t-shirt. Casey pouted and Daniel leaned over to kiss her quickly before she could start bitching. "I know," he said with a smile. "You own me tomorrow. All day, I promise." Daniel turned his gaze to Lucky. "Coffee date later this week, Lucky Penny?"

Lucky's smile never faded. "Count on it, Billy Bob." She stood, reaching across the table to grab his straw cowboy hat that had earned him the nickname. She handed it to him "You almost forgot this. See ya later." Lucky waved at Daniel and Casey, the three of them quickly leaving Sacred Grounds.

"I'll text or call tomorrow morning," Daniel said with a palpable feeling of disappointment that Lucky was gone. He grinned disarmingly at Casey before they parted ways outside the coffee house.

∞

Dusk had come to Rancho Tehama and she was walking around the Tehama shopping district, stopping to look in windows at the fashionably dressed mannequins. He had spied her about ten minutes ago and couldn't look away. His blood pumped faster through his veins and if he could have cut himself to experience more of a rush, he would have, right then and there. He had other ladies to visit, of course, but Lucky was special. He couldn't wait to watch her take her last breath as he stabbed the life out of her. *Patience makes for a better adventure,* he reminded himself. He felt the vertigo coming on and knew that a blackout was imminent. His head was swimming and his vision blurred. Reluctantly, he turned his back on her and left using one of the side alleys.

∞

Daniel reclined on his big bed, the sound of Biggie Smalls blasting through the earbuds of his iPod. He had been working all afternoon on the dreaded chore list his dad had left on his desk that morning. He was turning over onto his back when he saw her sitting on the edge of his bed, smiling serenely.

"Greetings, Daniel. I'm Jayden Kinlan and I'm here to keep things running smoothly." She sounded almost cheerful. She was an older blonde woman, perhaps early 50's with a calm and direct gaze.

"How did you... who are you?"

"You know, you could search your mind as far back as you can and still not find me there because I've never appeared to you. I just sort of handled things from my part of the world." She shrugged, still smiling. "I'm your creator, Daniel. You live in my fictional world."

Daniel leapt up from the bed, backing up towards the bedroom door.

"Whoa, whoa! Lady, I don't know how you got in, but I think you need to leave quietly now. If you need help, I can call for help."

"As sure as the bed that I'm sitting on was not real, I made you, Daniel Hughes. I created you and everything in this world in prose form on my computer in the den of my home in Caddo. You see, Caddo is real and Rancho Tehama is fiction. You are all, however, a reflection of my real world." She shook her head, lost in thought for a moment. "I'll never really know when you became real, living, breathing entities."

"So, you're saying that none of this exists outside of a book? I'm just a character?"

"Bingo!" Jayden tapped her nose. She held out one delicate hand and a rose appeared in her palm. "To prove it to you." She lay the rose on the bed.

"Oh, God! I'm about to lose it," Daniel said loudly, rubbing his temples in shock. "I'm real." He looked at both hands for a moment. "You created me in your head but something made me real."

"People have said things about the strangeness of Caddo over the years, but I always listened with half an ear. Until I started writing the Mad World series and you all came to life. I have visited Rancho Tehama many times by just writing myself here. You are now a flesh and blood human being with free will. I swear, sometimes I come back to my computer after taking a break and you have done something that I would never write." She laughed gaily then sobered. "You've got to go, kid. Pack up what you need 'cause I'm writing you out of Rancho Tehama. There's a danger here with the Baby Doll Killer skulking."

His first thought was his family and Lucky. "How long will I be gone?"

"For quite some time. I'll write you into someplace safe," Jayden assured him.

"I feel batshit crazy for packing a bag and bailing with you, but I'm going to do just that because I have a gut feeling it's the right thing to do," Daniel said, heading to his closet. "According to you, I don't exist outside the pages of a book so, what's the harm?"

∞

Fifteen minutes later, Daniel wrote his parents a note, explaining that he needed to get away from Rancho Tehama for a while. He tacked the note on his mom's corkboard in the kitchen. He texted Lucky, basically giving her the same lame excuse, and it was the longest goodbye ever. Jayden had explained that no contact would be the best thing for right now. She led him to her expensive black car parked in the driveway and he loaded up his large bag.

Jayden gave him a brief, sympathetic smile and there was more than a little sadness in her eyes. She started the car, backed out of the driveway, and they headed out into the night.

∞

Summer, 2 Years Later

The night sky was a canopy of bright stars and the air was pleasantly warm in Rancho Tehama. Daniel took a few deep breaths as he headed through the town square to Sacred Grounds. Two years had passed, but all it took was a warm breeze to remind him of what had been and what had been lost. His parents were relieved by his return. It was good to be home.

Jayden had written a whole new life for him in another fictional community, complete with new friends and new dreams to follow. What she hadn't done, at his request, was to write a new girlfriend for him. He didn't care if he never saw Casey again, but finding Lucky was still his prime objective.

He saw her through the window of the coffee shop almost immediately. He felt comforted by the fact that being there was still a ritual. His heart was thumping like mad, but he didn't hesitate to walk into Sacred Grounds and approach Lucky's table. She looked up from her book and smiled. Her smile faded when she realized who he was.

"Hey, Lucky Penny. Been a long time," Daniel said quietly, smiling. He rubbed his bristled chin. "May I sit down?" He sat down in a chair across from her.

"Sure. There's no assigned seating in here," Lucky snapped. "Why did you leave so abruptly, Daniel? I called constantly and exploded your cell phone with texts but... nothing from you. And now you're just back?"

Daniel impulsively reached over, catching a few long strands of dark hair in his hand. "Your hair is still beautiful," he said softly. "You're wearing it longer now."

"Don't try to derail the conversation. And hair can do a lot of growing in two years," Lucky said defiantly. "Why did you leave? Where have you been? I thought we were close, but I guess I was wrong." Tears formed in her eyes and she dashed them away with a swipe of her hand.

Daniel spoke carefully, deciding to keep his explanation brief. This wasn't the time or place to reveal everything.

"I had to hit the open road and see what life was like outside of this town. I... I guess I wanted to explore before going on to the university." He paused, staring into her eyes. "What's your UC Berkeley story? Did you transfer from the college here and go on to the university?"

Lucky nodded. "Yes, I graduated three weeks ago and immediately packed up and came home. I don't share your enthusiasm for exploring life outside of the confines of this town. I've been working as a teacher's assistant for a while. I need to figure out what to do with my fancy degree." A small smile curved her lips and she covered his hand with hers. "I can't seem to stay angry with you. I'm happy that you're home."

Daniel was relieved that seeing Lucky again had been relatively painless. She was never one for dramatic scenes, but this whole thing could have gone horribly wrong. *It still could,* he thought darkly. Jayden had instructed him to tell Lucky the truth about their origins because she thought it would be easier for Lucky to hear it from him.

"Where are you staying now?" he asked.

"I'm renting a room in a big house along with two other girls. I live a few blocks from the town square," she replied.

"Can we go there, maybe? There are some things that I need to tell you and I'd like to do it somewhere less public."

She nodded in understanding. "That would be better." They both stood and headed for the front door of the coffee house. "Casey forgot about you after a while and gave the clothes that you left at her place to the Goodwill," she blurted out. "She's been dating someone else for a long time."

Daniel laughed. "I expected nothing less," he said as they walked out into the warm night.

∞

"So, what you're saying is that everybody here in Rancho Tehama is a... character in some writer's book?" Lucky said, disbelief evident in her tone.

Daniel and Lucky sat side by side on a small black sofa in her bedroom. Not knowing any other way to tell her the truth, he had spilled everything to her, tripping over his words. He decided to go with the best course of action. He extended an upturned hand to her and willed a red rose to appear in his palm.

Lucky almost fell off the sofa, shocked. She caught herself and met his eyes with amazement in hers. "How are you doing that?"

"Jayden, I need you," Daniel yelled.

A few moments went by and nothing happened. Suddenly, a single word written in red lipstick began to appear on Lucky's mirror.

"Believe," Lucky whispered in wonder. She turned to Daniel and embraced him tightly. "I thought you had lost your mind, telling me all that. But this is real. I don't know how, but it just is. With a computer keystroke, this Jayden could wipe out illness and death for everyone in Rancho Tehama. I have so many questions."

Daniel caught her face in his hands. "This is something that I have wanted to do for a very long time. Questions can wait." He kissed her. Her lips parted for him and he stroked her tongue with his. He had deliberately caught her unprepared, but now she seemed to be into it. She affectionately bit his bottom lip.

Their clothes hit the floor a few moments later, and when they were stretched out on her bed naked, Daniel finally knew what it was like to have a dream come true. Lucky showed him with her body what her mouth couldn't say. He caressed her everywhere and she eagerly welcomed his touch. He was between her legs, bringing wave after wave of pleasure. They made love until they were exhausted and Lucky drifted off to sleep in his embrace.

He didn't sleep, instead watching the gentle rise and fall of her breasts as she slumbered. He thought it best to leave her and go back to his parents' house. He wrote a note asking her to meet him at Sacred Grounds tomorrow night. He intended to answer as many of her questions as he could. Jayden only visited their world when absolutely necessary, preferring to let her characters make their own decisions and solve their own problems. She had told Daniel that her books for the Mad World series almost wrote themselves. He left the note on Lucky's desk and she slept on.

∞

The next night, Lucky walked on the same path as she always had, stopping to admire the new dresses in the same store windows. He watched her intently. Predictability would be her downfall. She crossed the town square, heading for Sacred Grounds. He knew he had to act fast. She walked past the alley where he hid and took out a big knife from the folds of his navy blue hoodie.

He leapt from the shadows, catching her from the back. She screamed before he could stop her and he clamped a hand over her mouth. This would be done with her back to him, he decided. An unwelcome thought in his head whispered, "Why don't you want her to see your face?"

Lucky was tough, but he was stronger. They struggled for a few moments before he brought the knife down, planting it firmly in her back with a solid *thunk*. He tried to catch her as she fell face down to the ground. As her life slipped away, she lifted her head to see her killer.

"No," Lucky said, sobbing. "Not you. Daniel...." Blood poured from her mouth and she coughed. She closed her eyes and was still.

Daniel could hear Lucky talking to him from some far off distance, but he couldn't answer. He was blacking out, becoming the other one again. He fought it, clutching his head, but the other one began to surface. Suddenly, Daniel was aware of his surroundings and he saw her sprawled on the ground in the alley. He looked down at the knife in her back in horror.

"God, no! Not me. I can't have done this," Daniel shouted. "Jayden, help me!"

Jayden appeared in the alley, tears rolling down her face. She rushed to Lucky, kneeling down with a keening sound.

"I'm sorry, baby," she whispered, stroking Lucky's hair. "I tried to keep you, above anyone else, safe."

"You knew about me, didn't you, Jayden? You knew that I was crazy, capable of anything. Why didn't you kill me off years ago?" He punched a wall, enraged.

"I had to be sure that you were the Baby Doll Killer before I did anything. I can't seem to control this side of you when I write. The murders just appear on my computer screen and I'm powerless to stop them. I hoped that it wasn't you, Daniel." She shook her head in sorrow. "My little Lucky is gone, but I will never give up on trying to bring her back."

"Kill me off now," Daniel said softly. He couldn't hold back the tears.

Jayden shook her head. "No," she said decisively. "You have a purpose and you're not done living quite yet. You're going to get into your car and drive right back to the home that I put you in. I'll handle everything else. Go. Now."

Daniel kneeled down and kissed Lucky's forehead. He stroked her hair before standing up, walking toward the town square without a backward glance at his best friend's body and Jayden, his creator.

∞

Caddo, Two Days Later

Jayden Kinlan lived for two things: her writing and her long dead daughter, Lucky. Her daughter was a victim of a hit and run car accident many years before, and breathing life into Lucky McCall, a fictional character, seemed fitting. Now they were both gone and she was desperate to find a way to bring her make-believe daughter back to life in make-believe Rancho Tehama. She planned on writing a few more novels for the Mad World series so she had time to set things right in her fictional town. Time was all she had left.

She sat at her desk, putting last minute touches on her latest Mad World novel. She wrote the final words: "As Daniel drove fast in the night, trying to put as much distance between himself and Rancho Tehama as possible, something miraculous happened in the Rancho Tehama morgue. Lucky McCall, deceased as of a few hours earlier, took a deep breath and opened her eyes."

Jayden left her computer to get a piping hot cup of coffee from the kitchen. When she returned to her den, a new sentence had appeared on her screen. Her heart raced and she moved closer to the computer screen. She read: "Lucky was disoriented, but she sat up just fine."

Jayden smiled, tears forming in her eyes. Her plan to bring Lucky back had worked. *Maybe Daniel can be fixed with more in-depth character development,* she thought dryly. For now, the two lovers would remain separated. Rancho Tehama was created to be a disturbing little suburb. *Why worry about it tonight?* she asked herself. She shut her computer down for the night and went outside to sit on her porch under Caddo's starry night sky.

Cushion

"This can't be happening," Carin Bell murmured to herself, surveying the wreckage of her new white BMW as the flames consuming it leapt high into the air and crackled. She took in the twisted hunk of metal with a body still inside. *My body,* she thought in horrified dismay. She was standing a few feet from the driver's side that she thought she had safely emerged from a few moments ago, and she felt as real and solid as any other person. She lifted a hand to see a disturbing glow emanating from her skin.

A wail erupted from her throat and she wrapped her arms around her middle and wept brokenly. To be so close to happiness in this life and to have it ripped away from her was more than she could bear. The new book she had slaved to write, the new car, her fiancé… all of it was gone for good and worth nothing now.

The paramedics and fire trucks arrived at the scene of her accident and the first responders swept past her and converged on the burning car. An officer approached her and asked her to step back onto the sidewalk with the other gawkers. As he was speaking, Carin nodded but her mind was working furiously. *He can see me,* she thought. *For whatever reason, he can see me.*

She was only three minutes down the street from her home in the quiet California suburb of Pasadena and she began to walk away from the scene in that direction. She needed to sit down and think things through or do whatever the hell ghosts did.

∞

The anger came right around the time that she settled down on her living room sofa. She had let herself in with the spare house key that she kept under the potted plant on the back porch. Her fiancé, Victor, would move on and marry someone else. She wasn't particularly close to her parents and they had other adult children who they cared about more. She wouldn't be grieved too long by anybody, she imagined. That left one person on this earth that she could reach out to – Billy Chambers.

Carin punched a throw pillow, grunting in frustration. She thought in writing the book, fiction with touches of factual experiences from her early life, that she would be free of the curse of Billy. *Nope,* she thought, still pissed. The idea came to her suddenly and it was magnificent. He probably wouldn't, even with her book's success, remember her in life, but Billy Chambers damn sure wouldn't forget her in death. It would take some careful planning over the next few days and she didn't know how long ghosts could hang around with the living, but she was an unstoppable train off the rails.

∞

That had been pitifully easy. Her assets hadn't been frozen yet so she still had some time to play. Billy Chambers, famous pop star icon, lie stretched out in the back seat of Carin's jet black rental SUV, passed out from the chloroform she had slipped over his nose while he had been taking a piss in the men's room of the seedy dive bar he frequented in Hollywood. She had made a big show out of helping him outside, explaining with a charming smile that he'd had one too many. *Amazing,* she thought. He's still doing the same thing after twenty years.

Carin smiled darkly. *Now comes the real fun....*

∞

"Arise, Billy Chambers," a soft voice whispered into his ear. His eyes were closed, but he could hear just fine. He felt hungover, his thoughts swirling in confusion. His mouth was cottony, filled with the foul aftertaste of something strong. As he struggled to open his eyes and rise up, he realized that his arms were tightly bound. The restriction of movement woke him up quickly.

The woman who had whispered in his ear was standing over him, a smirk on her pretty face. Billy had a thing for details and he took her and his surroundings in carefully. He noted that they were in a cheap motel. He had seen plenty of these in his long, illustrious career as a womanizer. Every piece of furniture in the depressing room was a functional brown. He was bound to a bed that had seen better days. Finally, he turned his big brown eyes to the woman. She was medium height, olive skin, and slender with long brown hair and a great rack. Her face was better than average, but she was no supermodel. *A pop star's life in LA,* he mused.

Billy jerked at his restraints and sighed. "Okay, fun's over. I got wasted and you fucked Billy Chambers. You now have some great memories and we're done here. Any pictures of my naked ass show up in the tabloids, I will not hesitate to sue you."

The woman's eyes narrowed as she stared him down and he felt like squirming. *Something's wrong here,* he thought as she moved even closer to him, getting right down in his face.

"I stopped expecting anything good from you years ago," she said suddenly. "You were bullshit twenty three years ago and you're bullshit now."

"Did we meet before last night? I meet so many girls. What, did I fuck you and leave you then, too?" Billy's laugh was snide.

The woman appeared infuriated and Billy wasn't surprised when her hand shot out and smacked his face hard. She grasped both sides of his face.

"Such a beautiful man but so ugly on the inside." She squeezed his face. "A phenomenal waste of talent and time." She ruffled his head of short, curly brown hair.

She grabbed a bottled water from the nightstand, untwisted the top, and raised it to his lips. He hurriedly gulped at the water, relieved to be rid of the taste in his mouth. She smiled darkly at his sloppy efforts to down it all before quickly taking the bottle away. "You're experiencing the aftereffects of chloroform."

Billy's eyes narrowed. "Oh, this is crazy. You had to drug me to get me to sleep with you?" He struggled to remember events from the night before and came up largely blank. He began to frantically pull against his ties. "Let me out of this, you insane bitch!"

The woman sat down on the edge of the bed, smiling with satisfaction at his panic. "My name is Carin Bell, Billy, not insane bitch. Although this is admittedly one of the craziest things I've ever done. But I had to get your attention somehow. Big star like you deserves some grand gesture like this." She leaned over and smacked his face hard again. "And, my name is definitely not Cushion!"

Billy frowned in confusion. "What?"

Carin nodded as if his response had been expected. "I knew you wouldn't remember. You and your creep-ass friends slash band mates have screwed your way around the world so why would you remember a fat, unattractive girl like me." She paused, taking a deep shuddering breath. Her eyes teared up and she shook her head slowly. "Unbelievably, there was a time when your boy band, All 4 U, was my whole life. You, Billy, were my whole life."

Billy's laughter was loud and mocking. "All of this because I wouldn't fuck you 'cause you were a fatty after a concert over twenty years ago? If I weren't tied up, I'd call all of my friends to tell them this crazy shit." He relaxed against the headboard, feeling more comfortable in the situation. He had dealt with many obsessed fans and groupies over the years and, while this was a bit extreme, he knew how to handle this one.

His voice softened and his eyes went all puppy-soft. "Carin, what you looked like twenty years ago isn't important. Look at you now, all gorgeous and everything. Untie me and we can get down to doing something about your obvious sexual frustration."

Carin stood, turning her back to him.

"But it *is* still important to me, Billy." Her voice was choked with emotion and he felt a twinge of guilt. "My friends and I spent so much money following you from city to city, hanging out with your entourage after concerts and at your hotels just to get close to you guys. One night, my friends and I got an invitation to party with you all in your hotel room. The other girls with me were gorgeous and you spent the whole night telling them that." She whipped around, her face angry and bitter. "Do you know what I got from you, Billy? The nickname, Cushion!"

Billy's laughter escaped before he could control it and he tried to close his mouth.

"Cushion? As in, 'more cushion for the pushin?' Carin, I was a kid... and a dick. I was good-looking and rich and I did awful things and said mean things without thinking." He sighed. "Untie me and I'll make it up to you." His eyes traveled the length of her body, taking in the fitted jeans that displayed a nice pair of legs and a great ass. "Gladly, make it up to you."

Suddenly, the bottled water smacked him square in the face and the long mirror on the bathroom door splintered. He looked on in shock as a chair flew across the room, smashing against the wall next to him. "What the fu—"

Carin began to sob in earnest when everything went still again.

"I would love to, Billy, but I'm dead. I finally achieved almost everything I wanted to in life. I lost the weight, got engaged to a good guy, and I even wrote a book about my experiences with All 4 U." She dashed the tears away with a quick hand. "It's fiction, of course, and in my book, I get to be the beautiful one. I did all this and before I could get married and enjoy my life and success, I died in my new BMW!"

Billy chose his next words carefully. The stuff flying around the motel room was enough to make him believe in the supernatural, but the fact that Carin was becoming increasingly transparent cemented his belief. He had spent so many years chasing his mother in death through mediums and tarot readings and now... he knew there was an afterlife.

"Good God, ghosts are real." His voice was soft with wonder.

"Yes, we are. My time here is short but I want something from you, Billy Chambers."

"Then you can, uh, what? Pass over in peace or something?" He nodded, his heart thumping. He was in the presence of something otherworldly and, for the first time, he truly looked at Carin. She was beautiful and probably always had been underneath all that weight. He had just been too young and dumb to appreciate her. She was also fiery. He was growing to like her more by the second. "I'll help you if you do something for me."

"What do you want?" Carin asked, crossing her arms.

"If you see her in the afterlife, tell my mom I love her." Billy fought back tears. "Just that, okay?"

Carin nodded. "I'll pass along your message. I want you to read my book and post an honest review on my website. Like it or hate it – I don't care. Just be honest. Then, I want you to sit back with a beer and try to remember who I was in life. You may not recall all of the times you were cruel to me at the hotels, but I do. I want you to reflect on what made you such a dick. Then, be a better person, Billy."

Carin was rapidly fading and, as she waved her hands, the ties fell away from Billy's arms, freeing him. He was up like a shot, arms outstretched to pull her into a fierce hug. He could barely feel her but she reached up, grabbing his face and kissing him soundly.

"I waited twenty-three years for that kiss." She sighed, smiling brightly for the first time. "Be a good guy, Billy. The world is already full of dicks."

"I'm sorry you're gone, Carin. And I'm sorry about naming you Cushion."

"Don't just be sorry. Be better."

With a flash of bright light, she was gone and Billy was alone. A single tear slid down his cheek and he brushed it away. He noticed his old jeans and t-shirt folded neatly in a chair in the corner by the television. He dressed quickly before reaching into his back pocket for his cellphone. He would need a ride from the motel and his driver and personal assistant was available twenty-four hours a day for such occasions.

"I need you to pick me up," Billy spoke into the phone. His tone was friendly, his heart feeling lighter than it had in years. "But first, I need you to grab me a beer and grab the new book by Carin Bell from the bookstore."

∞

One Year Later

Billy sat in the back of his lush SUV, the glass shield up to prevent any conversation between him and his driver. He wasn't being unfriendly, but he needed to decompress. He was traveling from Carin's university campus, where she had graduated from many years before with honors. He hoped he had done her proud today, even though a lot of what he said had been bullshit.

He had given a speech in which he had presented their friendship in the best possible – and least offensive – light before announcing that he was establishing the Carin Bell scholarship for eligible English majors. He knew that Carin was exceptionally gifted in English. After having that beer over a year ago after the night she had disappeared in his arms, he began to remember a lot of things about her. He also reflected on who he had been and how pathetic it was that he hadn't grown up the slightest bit in twenty years.

Carin had told him to man up and be better, and now he was. Billy Chambers was no longer living to be a Hollywood bad boy, more famous for his exploits than for exhibiting any true talent. For the first time in a long time, Billy was a real musician and his songs resonated with deep sadness and haunting reflection.

"Thank you, Carin," Billy whispered, hoping she could hear him wherever she was. He pulled his shades down to cover his eyes and watched the rippling ocean out the window as he rolled on.

Rock

Vanessa Chase sped along the sidewalk on her bike, long, curly ponytail whipping in the wind as she passed house after house on her block. It was late afternoon and sunny in Lawton, Oklahoma where she lived with her mom, and she knew she had precious few minutes left to have fun.

She traveled further along, looking back over her shoulder briefly to see if her mom was looking for her. Seeing no one standing on the porch of their little white house, she continued on to the end of the block and beyond, to where the abandoned buildings of old downtown Lawton stood ramshackle.

It didn't take long for Vanessa to spot something to occupy her last remaining moments of outdoor play. A big grey cat took cautious steps on the sidewalk across the street, eyeing her. Vanessa came to a stop on her bike, resting it on the broken concrete. She pulled the paper towel wrapped bacon strips from her jeans pocket and carefully crossed the street, making comforting sounds. She laid one bacon strip down on the ground in front of the cat.

The cat took careful nibbles of the bacon, mewling in hunger. Quickly, Vanessa grabbed the cat around the neck and began to squeeze its throat, closing off the air. The cat howled in fear and pain as she shook it roughly back and forth until its neck snapped, a little smirk on her angelic face.

"Don't you know by now never to trust strangers, you dumb cat?" She spoke the words softly and threw its lifeless body to the ground.

The sun was beginning to set, a vivid ball of fire in the late afternoon sky, and she knew her mom would be looking for her shortly. Vanessa gave the dead cat another kick with one tennis shoe before climbing on her bike and heading for home.

∞

Vanessa stood at the sink in the small bathroom, washing up for dinner. She ran the soapy washcloth across her face, stopping to stare for a moment at her reflection. At ten years old, she still favored her dad, who had been dead coming on three years. She had taken his green eyes and snub nose, her full lips and dark, curly hair coming from her mom. She looked away from the mirror to see her mom, Ellie, standing in the doorway wearing a gentle smile.

"Dinner's on the table waiting, Ness," Ellie said. "I'm glad you made it in today before dark. I know you're getting older now, but I just feel safer with you close to me in the evenings. Before too long, you'll be dating and then what will I do?"

Vanessa hunched her shoulders up with an innocent grin. "I'll make all the boys bring me home on time, I guess."

Ellie laughed. "Your grandpa's coming tomorrow to see us."

Vanessa nodded, wringing out the washcloth and hanging it on the shower bar. "We haven't seen him in a while. It's not the same as... before dad died."

Ellie stepped forward, catching her only child in a tight embrace. "I know, ladybug." She kissed her hair softly. "That just means that we ladies gotta stick even closer together."

Vanessa returned the hug, but her cold gaze remained fixed on her reflection in the mirror.

∞

After a pleasing dinner of meatloaf and mashed potatoes, Vanessa kneeled beside her bed to say her nightly prayer, as her mom insisted. She waited until Ellie's footsteps echoed down the hall to begin.

"Dear old man in heaven, I'll kill as many things as I want to," Nessa whispered venomously with clasped hands. "Amen."

Having kept her promise to her mom, Vanessa slid between her warm bedcovers, smiling.

∞

"Come give your grandpa a hug, Little Bit. I know it's been a long time."

Vanessa dutifully wrapped her arms around her grandfather as he kissed her forehead. She didn't know why he even pretended to love her anymore. Everyone knew, especially her, that any family love her grandpa, Grey, had for them was gone after the death of Vanessa's father, his only son.

"It's good to see you, Grandpa," Vanessa said, putting far more excitement into her voice than she actually felt. This old man could die tomorrow and she wouldn't really care. She curved her lips into what she hoped was a loving smile. She turned to Ellie.

"Mom, can I go ride my bike? You and Grandpa should talk."

Ellie nodded. "Yes, that's fine. Just home before dark, as usual. Also, the neighbors to the east of us and down the block are both looking for their cats. They haven't seen them in a few days and they're worried. Keep an eye out."

Vanessa kept her expression blank, even as her heart jumped a little. "Okay." She shot past them both, slipping out the screen door. She completely missed Grey staring after her with narrowed eyes.

∞

She was gonna do it, she decided after a few moments of surveying little Timmy Loftin playing with his fire truck on the sidewalk across the street. Vanessa had been riding aimlessly up and down the block for the past ten minutes when the five year old boy with the red curls caught her attention.

Vanessa rolled her bike over to stand right above Timmy, smiling at him as he looked up.

"Hi, Timmy. Wanna play? I know something much more fun than that toy you have."

"Hi, Vanessa." Timmy wiped the sweat beading his brow away with one hand. "Okay. What?"

Vanessa leaned down. "I'll take you to the old buildings on the back of my bike." She whispered the words excitedly, as if she were sharing some super-secret, important information that should stay just between the two of them.

Timmy's face lit up.

"Sure!" He jumped to his feet, grabbing up the small fire truck with one dirty hand. Vanessa held the bike steady as the boy climbed onto the back, clutching the toy with one hand and wrapping his arm around her waist to hold on. She pedaled away down the block toward the abandoned buildings.

∞

They had been playing inside one of the larger old buildings for close to a half-hour when Vanessa felt like the time was right. Timmy was seated in an old shopping cart that she had been wheeling him around in, laughing as he giggled when they hit the bumps. She had earlier spotted a good-sized rock that should take care of some business.

"Let's go look out that broken window," Vanessa suggested. "We can probably see our block from up here." She helped Timmy out of the cart and, taking his hand, led him over to the window. "Don't touch that glass. It'll cut you good."

"Wow, Vanessa! I can see everything up here." He gave her a gleeful smile before turning his attention back to the view of the neighborhood spread out below.

Vanessa slipped away from his side and carefully picked up the rock. She approached Timmy silently from behind, tuning out his excited chatter. She was totally focused on her dark task. He was turning to look at her when the first blow struck him dead center in his forehead. His expression was both pained and dazed, as if he couldn't quite understand what was happening.

Vanessa brought the rock down hard again in the same place, noting the dent in his forehead and the blood beginning to gush from the wound. Timmy crumpled to the ground completely still, and she immediately jumped into action. Grunting with effort, she lifted his small body and dropped him into the shopping cart. She threw the rock through the broken window into the weeds below.

Satisfied in the extreme, Vanessa came down the stairs to the open gate exit of the building and stopped short when she saw her grandpa standing outside, his eyes focused directly on her. He looked at her for a few long moments before looking up at the broken window. Tufts of Timmy's red hair blew in the breeze, the rest of the body in the cart concealed in shadows.

Vanessa stood silent, her defiant expression making it clear she had no comment.

Grey spoke first, his voice quiet. "Your mama's looking for you 'cause it's getting dark." He gestured at the broken window above. "I can see you've been busy, though." He came closer to his granddaughter, his blank expression never changing. "Well, I reckon you have wicked heart, child."

Vanessa kept her face equally neutral. "Pretty much, Grandpa... pretty much."

Grey gave a sudden barking laugh. "I suppose, then, it's time to show ya my killing fields from my young days." He ruffled Vanessa's ponytail as she stared at him in open-mouthed disbelief. "You come from me and your daddy. Who else did you think you was gonna grow up to be?" He laughed again and Vanessa's heart lurched with joy at the unexpected discovery that he understood everything and must really love her.

"Ya go on home. I gotta clean up your mess just like I cleaned up so many of your daddy's messes." Grey jerked his head up in the direction of the window, his green eyes bright from some malevolent inner fire. "Be a good girl now and do what Grandpa just told ya."

"Okay, Grandpa," Vanessa chirped, hopping on her bike. She gave him a happy little wave as she pedaled away. The wind whipped her ponytail out behind her and she rang the little bell on the handlebars as she raced home.

Paper

"I can't wait to marry you."

It took that one string of words coming from her lying mouth to ignite Zach's anger. He had been annoyed with his fiancée for most of the evening because he hadn't wanted to go to the party in the first place. He was tired of the LA scene and the endless parties that came along with it.

Zach Guyler and Naomi Halpern had been engaged for the better part of three years and involved for a while before that. She had felt that the relationship was going nowhere fast and wanted the trophy ring that told the world, yes, he was hers for keeps. So, he gave her the damn ring in spite of his nagging doubts.

Naomi was staring at him expectantly, a small smile on her lips. "This is the part where you say, 'Me, too.'" As he closed the front door of their modest apartment and shrugged off his jacket without saying a word, Naomi continued to stare at him. "Zach?"

He turned to face her, taking in the long dark hair that framed a pretty face with deep brown eyes. Naomi was the picture of innocence, but he knew better. He wasn't a stupid guy, but even the smart ones make mistakes. He had lost his head with his heart and wasn't sure, at this point, if recovery from this situation was even possible.

Zach's lips curved into a smile, but he was still angry. In fact, his gut burned and his head was pounding with the effort it took to restrain himself from lashing out at her. *Not yet,* a small voice whispered in his mind. Zach stood at about six feet, muscular with dark hair and arresting green eyes. He was more than attractive and devastatingly charming. He used this to his advantage without a shred of guilt. He used it now.

"Mrs. Zach Guyler? Sounds good to me." He even leaned in to kiss her and Naomi wrapped her arms around his neck. *What a fucking outstanding performance,* he mentally applauded her.

"Let's get down and dirty right now," Naomi whispered in his ear, stroking his stubbly chin. He leaned back and looked down at her with a grin, rubbing her neck gently.

"I'd like that," Zach whispered, placing his hand in the small of her back to guide her to their bedroom down the hall. The thought of being buried deep inside of her luscious body made him hard immediately, but his mind was somewhere else, somewhere much darker. In the end, Naomi had turned out to be no different than the others, so he would treat her like the others.

They entered the bedroom, tastefully decorated in shades of black and dark blue, and he flipped the lamp switch. She immediately began to strip off her little black dress, kicking off her heels. Her face was animated with anticipation as he unbuttoned his black shirt, tossing it carelessly to the floor.

"Lights on," Zach said. "I want to see every inch of you." She had her back to him, so he seized the opportunity to grab his trusty pocket knife and the handcuffs from a bottom drawer of his nightstand on the other side of the bed. He quickly shoved both items under a pillow, coming around to strip off his jeans.

Naomi was naked, sitting on the edge of the bed. She reached out a hand, pulling him to her. She cupped his erection in her soft hands and her smile was wicked. Looking down at her, he was incredibly turned on, but equally dispassionate. His disappointment in her had twisted into a burning rage and the love he'd had for her withered.

Zach knew then that there was no turning back and he really didn't want to. *Not time for second guessing,* the quiet voice whispered in his head. He grabbed both of her arms in his hands as he laid her back on the bed, pinning them above her head. He kissed her roughly, parting her lips with his tongue. He let go of her arms after she was trapped beneath the weight of his firm body and continued his sensual assault.

Zach cupped Naomi's breasts in his hands, stroking and kissing. His hands traveled the length of her body and his touch was rough and demanding. A part of him hated himself for still wanting her and he tried to control the anger and make himself stop. There was another part that knew he had to have her one last time.

He didn't stop her from stroking the length of his erection, making him harder. His breathing became uneven and he could feel himself losing focus, becoming lost in the moment with her. He suddenly snapped as she kissed his neck and he entered her deeply with one smooth stroke. As he began to move inside of her, he could hear her panting and whispering his name over and over. He grabbed her hips and wished for the familiar feeling of joy as they came together. He felt nothing in this moment but a need to finish this.

As soon as it was over, Zach moved across her quickly and grabbed the items under the other pillow. He had her handcuffed by one hand to the headboard in three seconds. Naomi tried to sit up quickly and jerked against the restraint. She laughed, shaking her head.

"The cuffs, tonight? You read my mind." She relaxed against the headboard. "Okay, I'm down for this if you are."

Zach got up from the bed holding the pocket knife and he grabbed the chair from the corner. He turned it around and sat down, his arms folded on top of the back of the chair. He clenched the sheathed knife, staring at her intently.

"Quite an interesting conversation you were having with Michael tonight, Naomi." He paused for a moment, remembering every earlier detail.

Naomi's expression never changed but he watched her tense up. "You know Michael, Zach. He doesn't think anything about those inappropriate party conversations. He's obsessed with his dick and wants the world to know it."

"But you would know all about his dick, wouldn't you?" Zach clipped the words out, his tone cold. He continued to smile. "You honestly believe that I didn't know you've been screwing him for quite some time? I lied to myself, tried to make excuses for you, but I have always known."

Naomi blinked in surprise. "Zach, no—"

"Bullshit. You're gonna lie, so I call bullshit on everything you say to me at this point. Don't say another word in your defense because I will take it as an insult to my intelligence. For months, you and Michael have been hooking up whenever and wherever you could while I was out busting my ass at work to provide for our life together. Bitch, you should be dead."

Naomi's lips twisted and she shook her head. "Typical Zach. So over-dramatic." She sighed deeply. "Okay, fine. I did cheat a few times, but you love me like I love you and you will come to understand that part of me and why I do the things I do sometimes. It's not like you're gonna kill me over this." She rolled her eyes.

Zach laughed at that, a hearty guffaw that came rumbling from his throat. He gave her a level look.

"Oh, I *am* gonna kill you." To show he meant serious business, he was out of the chair and slashing her thigh with the knife in one smooth movement. She cried out in surprise and pain, her eyes wide and tearing up. He was satisfied with her reaction and sat back down on the chair across from her.

"But first, Naomi, we're gonna talk all about what made you such a using, manipulative bitch and, overall, a bad girlfriend. If I like your answer to my first question, you won't suffer too much and I'll make sure your family has a body to bury."

Naomi began to scream and struggled against the cuffs. Zach stood up, covering her mouth with one big hand. He met her panicked eyes with his own.

"Okay, no answers from you, then? That's incredibly disappointing. I was really looking forward to some textbook-response explanation of why you turned out to be such a worthless whore." He put the knife to her neck. "Lights out, bitch." Zach slid the knife smoothly across her neck, severing arteries and ending her life instantly. Blood spurted from the gaping wound, drenching the sheets in crimson.

As a finishing touch, he took his time carving the word 'whore' on one of her supple thighs and removed the expensive engagement ring from her finger. He gave serious thought to his life of freedom without Naomi. She hadn't been the one, just like the others hadn't been, and he had dealt with her accordingly.

That didn't mean that it was time to give up. The woman who would be his perfect wife and mother to his future children was still out there. He obviously could no longer stay in LA, but that gave him the perfect opportunity for a fresh start somewhere new.

Is this happiness? He turned it over in his mind. Naomi had been stifling and oppressive, but would he come to miss her eventually? He doubted that. He didn't miss any of the others, so why would this time be any different? He decided, as he carefully began wrapping up her body, that happiness was relative. He was unlike anyone else, special even, and the rules of happiness that applied to most people didn't apply to him. So, it was time to disappear again.

Zach whistled a happy little tune as he worked. He had another body to get rid of.

∞

Six Months Later

Irma Irwin was about to be deeply sorry that she had messed with him. After Naomi's unfortunate end in LA, Zach had quickly fled the scene, heading up to Caddo, a small but thriving city in Northern California. Once settled in a tiny box of an apartment, he took a job as an administrative assistant in an average office with an average supervisor and worked every boring weekday for the standard eight hours, with a half-hour for lunch. Obviously, he knew that he was overqualified and underpaid, but his cash was running low. Caddo wasn't meant to be a forever home, anyway.

Zach carefully slipped the last item, a handgun, into the tote bag he had been packing for the past ten minutes. He was patient and meticulous in his planning, however. This had to go down right if it was going to go down at all. He double-checked the bag before zipping it closed. Perfect. He had everything he needed to get his point across.

Zach whistled a jaunty tune as he left his cracker box home, locking the door securely and heading down the hallway. He ran through his mental checklist and, confident that everything was in place with his plan, he came down the stairs and headed for his car.

∞

Zach had broken a window to get into the house and now stood in a dark corner of the living room. He could see the driveway from his position and kept checking it, waiting for her car to pull in. He leaned over and again went through the items in his tote bag. When he spied the large white envelope at the bottom, his head began to throb as his anger simmered. *Amazing how a few words on a page can change everything,* he thought, trying to keep his hands steady.

∞

Zach didn't have a long wait for Irma. Her car had pulled up into the little driveway a few moments before and he heard the click of the lock and the jangle of keys as she let herself into the house. A sliver of moonlight showed through the open front door as she struggled with her work bag.

He was on her the moment she closed the front door, stepping from the shadows. Irma let out a surprised bellow when blows from the butt of the handgun he held firmly struck her head and shoulders, immobilizing her for a few moments. She fell to the floor, trying to shield herself from the vicious pistol whipping. He seized the opportunity to roll her onto her stomach, jerking her arms back, and snapped the hand cuffs on.

Irma was simply average. Not tall and not short; not attractive but not ugly, with short brown hair. All of that mattered very little to Zach. What he hated her for most was for having average intelligence. She had thought she was superior to him and felt comfortable playing dictator to him and the other office folk he worked with eight hours a day. He had been amused for a while, but his good humor about the work situation quickly evaporated into a burning rage when he had read his six month job performance review.

Zach moved his supervisor from her position on the carpeted floor with a minimal amount of effort, shoving her down roughly onto her brown leather sofa before flipping the lamp switch. Irma blinked a few times before her eyes met Zach's, her lips parting slightly in surprise.

"You look confused, Irma," Zach said in a quiet voice, his lips curved into a congenial smile. He moved back to his hiding corner, grabbing his tote bag full of goodies just for Irma to enjoy. He came back to stand directly in front of her, shoving the gun under her chin to ensure her cooperation. Her expression was panicked. Her wild eyes rolled in terror and one particularly nasty gash on her forehead was beginning to drip blood down her cheek.

"If you move even the slightest bit in any way from that sofa, I will blow your head off," Zach explained, setting the ground rules. He stepped back from her. "You picking up what I'm laying down?"

Irma nodded vigorously, twin trails of tears running down her cheeks. Zach turned away from her, placing the gun within easy reach on a nearby chair, and pulled the white envelope out of his bag. He waved it at her before opening it and sliding a few sheets of paper out.

"Recognize this?" Zach's tone was cheerful. "You should. You wrote this crap performance review and even signed it." His eyes moved to her face, satisfied to see panic in her eyes.

"But, I didn't...."

"Don't interrupt me, Irma," Zach said in a clipped tone. "You didn't what? You didn't think they were gonna shitcan me?" He flipped through the pages in his hands for a brief moment. "Let's read some of this, shall we?" He looked up and smiled before he read. "'Zach is clearly not a good fit for our company. He seems unmotivated, even distracted at times. His work is sloppy and he is disorganized overall. He has a habit of making inappropriate comments to his female co-workers and appears to spend large amounts of time socializing as if our office is a nightclub. I do not give him high marks in any category and recommend termination of employment immediately.'"

Zach looked up from the page, shaking his head slowly. "You really are fucking clueless about who I am, aren't you? Words are cheap, so easy to let fall out your flapping lips and to put on a sheet of paper. But, you know what, Irma? You're gonna *eat* your words." He began tearing the page into strips and moved to where she sat on the sofa. Her eyes widened in fear as he grabbed her chin, forcing her mouth open. He shoved a few paper strips into her mouth. She gagged, trying desperately to close her mouth.

Zach used extreme force, shoving in a few more strips of paper.

"Your words were shit, Irma. In fact, they were an... an... explosion of shit coming from your big, stupid mouth. The thing to do here is to clean it up." He let go of her chin abruptly, watching with satisfaction as she struggled to breathe. His face was carefully blank as he dug through his bag, pulling out a roll of toilet paper.

Zach was on her in a heartbeat, pulling open her mouth again and forcing strips of toilet paper down her throat with three of his fingers. Irma's face was bloody and wet with tears. She was choking and flailing as he suffocated her. When he had filled her throat and mouth with paper, he stepped back and calmly watched her die. It took all of a minute and then it was over. Her eyes rolled back in her head and she fell over sideways on the sofa.

Zach allowed himself a grin. He had never been the type to just roll over and take the bullshit the world often handed him. He knew how to deal with a problem. He whistled a lively tune as he began to clean up the mess.

On to another city where true love is waiting, he thought. This had just been a rest stop. He had a good feeling, knowing that if he just stayed positive, happiness in the form of a good woman would soon follow. His heart was a patch of dirt right now, but soon love would bloom there, like a wild bush of roses. And he could wait. He had patience in spades.

Scissors

"These are perfect. I'll take them," Aldous Parker said, turning the pair of scissors over in his hands. They shone brightly even in the dim store, the gold trim on the handles gleaming. The saleslady smiled, nodding her approval.

"One of our hottest sellers. You've made an excellent choice, sir," she said. "Shall I have them gift wrapped?"

Aldous handed her the scissors, smiling politely in return. "That would be great." He handed her his credit card.

It was Christmas Eve again and he didn't know why he had expected his pain to subside. It had been a whole year since the accident, but he still thought of his daughter, little Michelle, every day. For her, there would be no anticipation of Santa's visit, complete with cookies left out. There wouldn't be any more tree decorating or caroling with the neighbors' children.

The saleslady returned, handing him his credit card and a small, decorative box. She wished him season's greetings and he thanked her, heading out of the store. At last, everything was in place for a somber Christmas Eve with his wife, Courtney. They lived in a beautiful house in an upscale part of Pasadena, but the joy of finally living well was gone.

Aldous headed home in his expensive Audi as the rain began to sprinkle a light mist on his windshield. *These are my tears for my baby girl,* he thought, his face twisting in sorrow.

∞

Aldous stared at his reflection in the bathroom mirror. He wore a pair of jeans and a simple black t-shirt. He was tall, with broad shoulders and a trim, fit body. His olive skin and dark, short curly hair had been turning heads since puberty and, at one time, he had greatly appreciated the feminine interest. All of that changed when he met and married Courtney five years before.

Courtney was a rich girl, coming from an affluent California family, in contrast to his middle class background. They had met shortly after Aldous had done his duty and served his country as a Marine. She was tall, blonde, and strikingly beautiful, but that wasn't enough to push him to actually want to marry and settle down. Their marriage was a result of an accidental pregnancy and she had insisted on having the ring and his last name. Skittish but in love, he had given her both.

Aldous noted the new crinkles and dark circles under his eyes as he tried to recall how many times he had cried over the past year when he thought of Michelle. Tears welled in his eyes and he dashed them away with the back of one hand. *All for you, baby girl,* he thought. He grabbed one of Courtney's hair brushes. He flipped off the light in the bathroom and headed downstairs for dinner.

∞

"Now that you have the table cleared, let's go into the living room so I can brush your hair like I used to," Aldous spoke to his wife with a gentle smile. She looked stunning in a short, black lounging gown.

Courtney smiled back, nodding. "That sounds perfect, sweetie." She went into the kitchen. "Let me grab a bottle of wine."

He was seated on one sofa when she came in with wine in one hand and two glasses in the other. She placed them on a nearby table and sat down on the carpet between his legs. He began brushing her long hair with firm strokes, stopping briefly only to massage her scalp. He looked to his side as he brushed. It was time to give her the gift.

"It's been a hard year," Aldous commented softly.

Courtney heaved a deep sigh. "I know, Al. Michelle's accident was tragic and painful, but we will have other children. No need to stop living completely." She patted his knee.

Aldous had opened the gift box while she was in the kitchen. He grabbed the expensive scissors from the box, clutched a hunk of her hair, and snipped it off down by the root. When she turned around, looking at him in confusion, he showed her the small bundle of hair.

"This is what it feels like to lose something precious to you, Courtney."

"What the…." She stopped midsentence when he grabbed her around the neck, shoved her forward, and drove the scissors deeply into her back. She let out a whoosh of air, trying to scream as she fell forward on her belly.

Aldous got down on his knees, leaning over her.

"From the moment she was born, you used my daughter to get whatever you wanted from me. You never loved her." He spat the words, rising to his feet. "Michelle was my everything, and now, because of you, I'll never see her again."

Courtney was panting and squirming, trying to make the pain stop. Her grunts echoed loudly in the large room and, through it all, Aldous stood silently watching.

"Do you even remember last Christmas Eve, Courtney?"

∞

Christmas, the Year Before

Michelle had Mommy's good scissors and was on the move. She was dressed in one of her cartoon footie pajamas, dark curly hair back in a ponytail. Mommy had been wrapping gifts all evening and had abandoned the task to take a cell phone call. She didn't know why Mommy was locked in the downstairs bathroom talking on her phone, but she was laughing a lot so it must've been Grandma. Daddy wasn't home yet, so she saw it as a good opportunity to grab the treasured scissors and make her Christmas picture for them.

She ran swiftly, cutting sharply around the corners and laughing excitedly. They would be so happy to see what she made for them! She approached the staircase at full speed and began to descend, without slowing down or grabbing the hand rail. As she came down quickly, she lost her footing suddenly and began to tumble, scissors in hand. She let out a terrified, pained shriek as she felt the scissors penetrate the soft skin of her belly. *Mommy, help me!* was her last thought as everything went black. She lay at the bottom of the stairs like a rag doll.

∞

Aldous pulled the scissors from his dying wife's back, rolling her over with one foot. Blood was dripping from her open mouth as she struggled to stay alive. She tried to speak but coughed up more blood.

"If you hadn't been talking to that asshole you were cheating with, Michelle would still be here. What the hell were you thinking, leaving a three year old to run around the house while you're barricaded in the bathroom?" He kicked her side viciously. "This was all your fault and I'm actually glad that you're gonna die tonight."

Courtney tried to curl her body into a tight ball and he kicked her. He kneeled down again, grabbing her by the hair.

"Scissors will be the last thing you ever see, just like Michelle." He plunged the scissors into Courtney's throat, killing her instantly. He watched the blood spurt for a moment before releasing her hair, letting her head fall back onto the carpet.

Aldous wasn't deluding himself. He knew that he would do hard time for this, but oh, had it been worth it. He felt completely justified in ending Courtney's life. Why should she be free to move on with life while his child lay cold in a grave? He whispered a little prayer for himself and Michelle before moving over to the sound system in the corner of the living room.

Aldous listened to the soft 70s soul music playing in the background and enjoyed a glass of wine, waiting for the ax to fall.

About the Author

Tamela Miles is a published horror and paranormal romance author, well known for her short stories and novellas. Her work also appears in the Independent Author Index Short Story Compilation, Volume 4.

She took first prize in 2011 from the "Voices of Compton Literary Journal," published by El Camino College, for her short story, "Breathe," which is included in her horror compilation, *Rock, Paper, Scissors*. Ms. Miles is a graduate student with a Bachelor of Science in Child Development. She also freelances as a child development advocate in her downtime, which she wishes she had more of. She welcomes the challenge and satisfaction of writing a good story and can't imagine doing anything else with her time. She loves all things horror and marrying it to romance in her work is always exciting. Romance is great, but add in a demon and Halloween's Michael Myers riding on the back of dragon and she's hooked.

She grew up in the chilly foothills of Altadena, California during the tumultuous but golden 1980s. She now comfortably resides with her family in the Inland Empire, California and often uses her view of the beautiful foothills in the area to inspire her as she stays planted in her chair to write. When she isn't busy unleashing her both frightening and steamy stories on unsuspecting readers, she is lost in reading books, watching true crime drama shows, and enjoying many genres of music.

You can visit her on her Facebook author page, Tamela Miles Books. She is always happy to hear from fellow readers and writers.

https://www.facebook.com/Tamela-Miles-Books-350618404965591/

Other Books by Tamela Miles

It's All in the Telling, 2011 by Tamela Miles
http://amzn.to/1RpnPtV

Sleeping Beauties, 2013 by Tamela Miles
http://amzn.to/1PHSe8q

If you enjoyed this book, please leave it a review on Amazon! Reviews not only help readers to find their next great book, but also help authors to improve upon their work when the feedback is constructive.

If you'd like to leave a review on Amazon, it would be greatly appreciated!

Thank you so much for taking a few minutes to help readers and authors!